Dragon Village
COLOBAR

RONESA AVEELA

BENDIDEIA
PUBLISHING

Contents

Characters iv
Glossary.. viii
Chapter 1 Somber Ritual 1
Chapter 2 The Search Begins.................................... 13
Chapter 3 Hideaways... 23
Chapter 4 The Cold Marsh....................................... 35
Chapter 5 Mysterious Wizards 45
Chapter 6 Discovery 53
Chapter 7 Secret Rendezvous.................................. 59
Chapter 8 A Mother's Love 71
Chapter 9 Reunion... 81
Chapter 10 The Power of Light................................. 89
Chapter 11 Danger in the Woods 99
Chapter 12 Prisoner 109
Chapter 13 Secret Weapon 119
Chapter 14 Battle Plans 131
Chapter 15 Warning from the Sky 141
Chapter 16 The Great Awakening........................... 155
Chapter 17 The Sacrifice... 165
Chapter 18 A Change of Heart................................ 175
Chapter 19 Light and Darkness.............................. 187
Chapter 20 Dragon Legacy...................................... 199
Chapter 21 Long Live the Queen 211
Chapter 22 Magnificent Dragons........................... 223
About the Author 233

Characters

Theo: Thirteen-year-old boy who has connections to Dragon Village.

Pavel: Theo's best friend who invents gadgets.

Diva: Samodiva girl who lives in Dragon Village. Diva's name means "wild." *Samodiva* means "Wild alone." From Bulgarian mythology, Samodivi were wild creatures who shied away from humans.

Baba Yaga: Witch from Slavic folklore who lives in a house with chicken feet.

Bendis: Thracian goddess of the moon, often said to be the mother of the Samodivi.

Bird of Paradise: Spirit birds, such as Sirin, Alkonost, and Gamayun.

Boo: A magpie.

Bor Stobor: A Karakonjul. *Bor* means pine in Bulgarian, and *stobor* is a strong person (strong like a big pine wood).

Celestial Turtle: A giant turtle from the mythologies of various cultures. It holds the world on its back.

Colobar (plural, Colobari): A priest of the god Tangra.

Dimana: A Rusalka who's hostile toward Theo.

Dracoville: A nickname Pavel gave Theo, combining his dragon and Samodiva heritages.

Drakus: An Oupir (vampire).

Firebird: In Slavic mythology, a bird that can be both a blessing and a curse. Its feathers glow brightly, and some say the bird can see the future.

Hala: Lamia and Zmey's mother. Female dragon who is associated with the wind and bringing storms.

Harpy: Half-woman, half-bird creature from Thrace and found in Greek mythology.

Ispolin (plural, Ispolini): Bulgarian word for "giants."

Jabalaka: The Keeper of Secrets. A man Lamia turned into a frog creature. *Jaba* is the Bulgarian word for "frog."

Jega: A Kuker (mummer) who wields fire. The word *jega* means "hot" in Bulgarian.

Karakonjul: Half-man, half-horse creature.

Kikimora: Creature who lives in the marsh, where she brews beer.

Knights of Darkness: Knights of Light who were corrupted by Zlo.

Knights of Light: Zmey's special guards who remained faithful.

Kobur: One of the Colobari.

Konedrakon (plural, Konedrakoni): A fictional mythical creature that is a combination of horse and dragon. *Kone* is "horse" in Bulgarian, and *drakon* is "dragon."

Kosara: Guardian of the Znahar Tree.

Kotka: Baba Yaga's flying cat. *Kotka* is the Bulgarian word for "cat."

Kuker (plural, Kukeri): A man who wears animal skins and huge bells that scare evil spirits. The tradition dates back to Thracian times.

Lamia: Zmey's sister. Female dragon with three dog-like heads. She is cruel and brings hail to destroy crops, as well as stopping the flow of water.

Lesnik: Kikimora's husband. A guardian of the forest.

Lora: Drakus' wife.

Lord Vodnik: Leader of the water creatures.

Lucky: One of Lord Vodnik's male water buffaloes.

Magda: Zunitza's sister.

Mora (plural, Mori): A type of demon that causes nightmares.

Mraz: The oldest of the Kukeri brothers. The Bulgarian word is for "cold."

Nav (plural, Navi): A demon that looks like a bird with a distorted infant's head.

Nia: Theo's twin sister.

Oupir: A type of Bulgarian vampire.

Pavel-dome: One of Pavel's inventions that shoots out electrical currents.

Radan: A warrior, Lord Zlo's second-in-command.

Rattan: One of the Colobari.

Rusalka (plural, Rusalki): Bulgarian word for water spirits, often called mermaids.

Ruslana: A Rusalka who's friendly toward Theo.

Samodiva (plural, Samodivi): Woodland nymph in Bulgarian lore. You may be more familiar with one of their other names: Veelas, like in the Harry Potter stories.

Sava: Diva's oldest sister.

Shar: Theo's deer companion. *Shar* means "colorful" in Bulgarian.

Sirin: One of the "birds of paradise," half-women, half bird. She sang beautiful songs that made listeners forget everything.

Sitara: Blacksmith. Former Vurkolak (werewolf) who once guarded one of Lamia's souls.

Sly: A Vodnik, friendly toward Theo.

Struma: Spirit of a woman built into a bridge wall.

Sur: Diva's deer companion. *Sur* means "gray" in Bulgarian.

Tagan: One of the Colobari.

Tangra: Thracian god of light and the sun.

Ula: Diva's sister.

Uroki: Evil spirit.

Vodna: Queen of the Rusalki.

Vodnik (plural, Vodni): Slavic water creature that looks like an old man or a frog-like creature.

Vurkolak: Bulgarian word for "werewolf."

Water Bull: Demonic creature, part bull, part fish, part human, that lives in Rabisha Lake.

Whirl: Pavel's deer companion.

Youda (plural, Youdi): Evil Samodiva who lives in forests and mountains. She has the power of witchcraft.

Youda Stana: The leader of the Youdi.

Zima: A Kuker who has the power of freezing. The word *zima* means "winter" in Bulgarian.

Zlo: Lamia's lord and mentor. The word in Bulgarian means "bad" or "evil."

Zmey: Theo's birth father. Villages throughout Bulgaria have invisible patrons who protect their villages.

Zunitza: A Samodiva. Theo's birth mother. The word comes from *zuna*, the Bulgarian for "rainbow."

Glossary

Chamber Room: Room in the castle where the Golden Apple is hidden.

Cherna Mountain: *Cherna* is the Bulgarian word for "black." This is where the dragon castle is found.

Chutura: An old Bulgarian word for "mortar."

Cold Marsh: Home of the Vodni, Jabalaka, and Kikimora.

Devil's Throat: A cave in the western Rhodope Mountains in Bulgaria, said to be the entrance to Hades.

Dracophone: Pavel's invention to call home to Selo.

Forest of Souls: The place where the souls of Dragon Village's ancestors reside in globes.

Forest of Whispering Bells: Forest where Baba Yaga lives. The bells jingle when someone approaches.

Golden Apple: In Slavic folklore, a fruit that has an association with the Firebird.

Horo: A circle dance.

Kadin Bridge: Called "Bridge of the bride" (*Kadin most*) in Bulgarian, or "Bride bridge" (*Nevestin most*), the Kadin Bridge is a stone arch bridge that spans the Struma River at Nevestino in southwestern Bulgaria. It was constructed in 1470.

Kaleto: The Forgotten Land, home of the Ispolini. In Bulgarian, the name means "fortress."

Kaval: Shepherd's pipe. A long, flute-like instrument that Samodivi like to dance to. They often make shepherds play the instrument until they drop dead from exhaustion.

Komuniga: Yellow sweet clover (*Melilotus officinalis*). Lethal to dragons.

Lamia's Bible: A book that contains secrets about those living in Dragon Village.

Magura Cave: A cave in northern Bulgaria where prehistoric paintings have been found. The cave is near Rabisha Lake.

Ouroboros: A snake or dragon swallowing its tail and forming a circle, symbolizing infinity.

Pavel-dome: One of Pavel's inventions that shoots out electrical currents.

Rabisha Lake: A freshwater lake in northern Bulgaria that legends say is the home of the Water Bull.

Rodina Forest: *Rodina* means "homeland" in Bulgarian. Named after a forest in the Strandja Mountains in southern Bulgaria.

Selo: Fictitious place along the Black Sea. Bulgarian word for "village."

Smil: Magical flower harvested in Dragon Village.

Surnitza: A town in south-central Bulgaria in the Rhodope Mountains. It is located near a semi-circle of rock structures that have been called a "snake city" due to the snake heads that have been hewn into the rocks.

Telkapan: One of Pavel's inventions. A net that captures demons. *Tel* means "wire" in Bulgarian, and *kapan* means "trap."

Vida: Village where Youdi and Sitara live.

Zandan: Prison in the dragon castle. Bulgarian word for "prison" or "dark place."

Zmeykovo: Bulgarian name for "Dragon Village." Mystical land where mythological creatures live. Said to be at the end of the world.

Znahar Tree: A fictitious World Tree connecting the three realms: heavens, earth, and underworld.

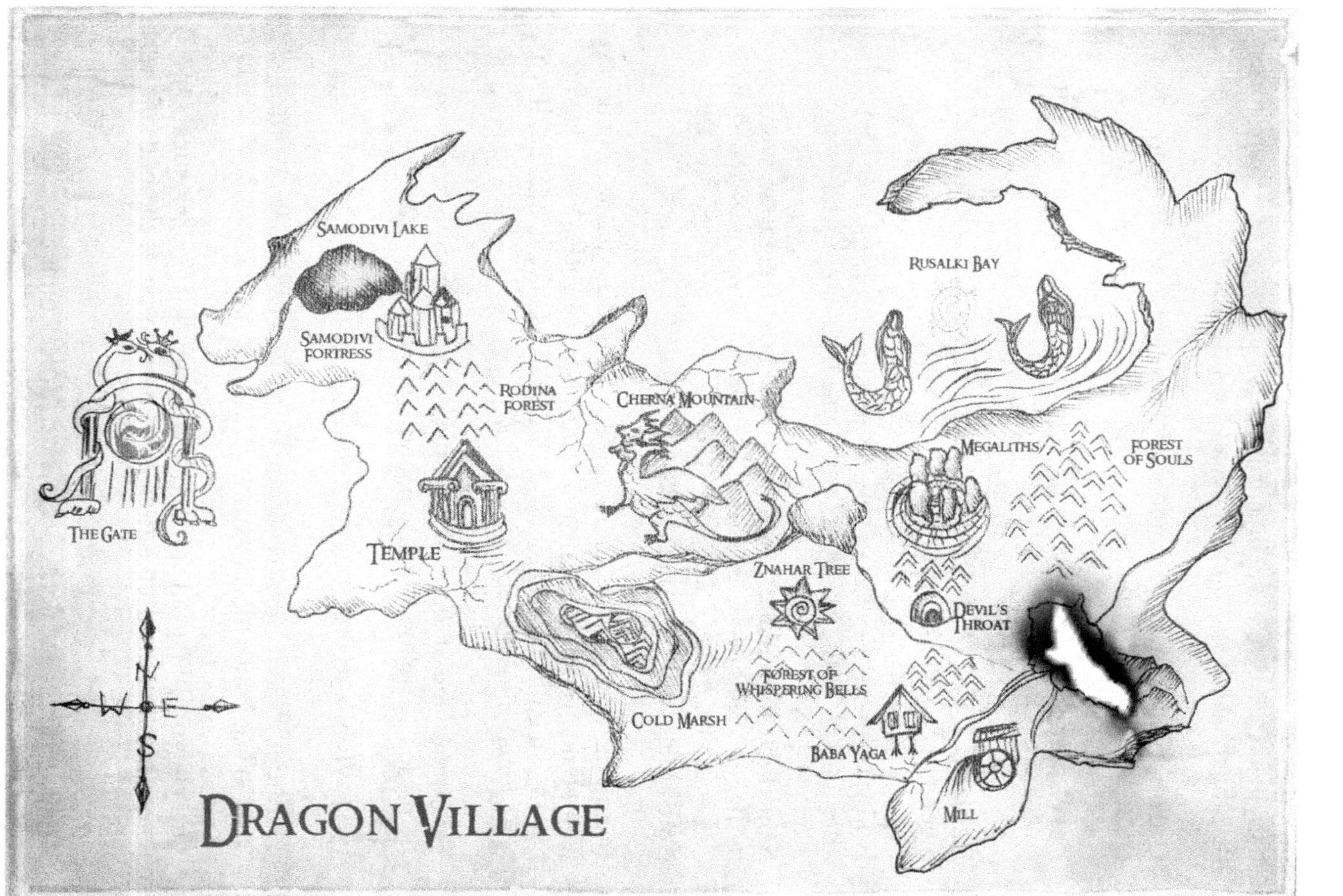

Samodivi Lake
Rusalki Bay
Samodivi Fortress
Rodina Forest
Cherna Mountain
Megaliths
Forest of Souls
The Gate
Temple
Znahar Tree
Devil's Throat
Forest of Whispering Bells
Cold Marsh
Baba Yaga
Mill
N W E S
Dragon Village

Chapter 1
Somber Ritual

JULY 12

THE ONCE VIBRANT WATERS of Samodivi Lake appeared to weep as a gentle breeze disturbed the still surface and sprayed its golden droplets over Diva like a shroud. She lay beneath a weeping willow that stretched toward the water's edge. A bed of the tree's slender branches, entwined with colorful flowers, enfolded her lifeless body like a mother's tender embrace.

In death, Diva's pale face resembled marble. A basil wreath encircled her wild curls, which had been braided to form a crown, acknowledging her newly discovered status of princess. Someone had thoughtfully clothed her in a clean, white robe, without any embellishments, replacing the blood-soaked garment, as if to erase the reminder of the battle they'd all only recently fought. However, Theo couldn't forget watching in horror as Lamia swung her sword-sharp tail and stabbed Diva in the chest. The girl he had come to know and love now looked like a frightened, fragile child, not the strong, brave warrior she had been.

With his shirt sleeve, Theo wiped away a tear that trickled down his cheek. He had changed out of his own bloody, battle-torn clothing to pay his last respects to the sister he had found and lost in the same moment. If only they had had time to embrace the fact they were family.

Theo wasn't the only one who mourned Diva's loss. At his side, his father gulped in air, and Theo tore his eyes away from Diva's face as Zmey stumbled toward the daughter he had never known he had, until it was too late. Pavel, as well as Diva's sisters, Sava and Ula, stepped aside to make room for the king of Zmeykovo to kneel at his child's side.

Zmey held Diva's hands. His voice cracked as he spoke. "My daughter. Zunitza, our lovely daughter. How could my sister do this to her? And your sister … Magda. Such betrayal. We showed them only love. The apple … the robe … could have revived our beautiful child. Now it's too late. She's gone to join you."

Theo clenched his hands into fists. The Golden Apple had the power to restore Diva's life. Now, it was missing. It had to have been Magda who stole it. She must have removed Zmey's key when he was sleeping—or when she'd intentionally made him unconscious. After Theo and his father had discovered the empty box where the apple had been, Zmey had raced to his bedroom and thrown open the cupboard where he kept Zunitza's wedding ensemble. Her robe and belt held Samodivi healing powers. But those items had disappeared. Magda had even taken Zunitza's wedding dress. His aunt had taken everything that could have restored Diva's lifeforce. Theo berated himself for returning the belt to the cupboard. He'd thought for certain Magda wouldn't dare touch it again, after pretending that Diva had stolen it the first time.

Blinking away tears, he glanced at the others who stood on the shore. The Samodivi had gathered around the magnificent weeping willow. Near the women, Jega with his Kukeri brothers stood tall, their spears thrust into the ground. The men wore ceremonial attire made from animal pelts, and heavy bells girded the men's waists. The Kukeri, too, had suffered the loss of one brother recently, while the eldest remained in hiding to keep the book of secrets hidden from Lamia. The men even believed that their father had perished. Theo knew the truth, but he'd sworn he wouldn't betray Jabalaka's secret, in order to keep the man safe.

Other friends huddled around, as well. Sitara and Drakus were both victims of Lamia's wrath and were desirous of revenge. Even the witch Baba Yaga had arrived in her broken-down Chutura, with the chicken-like being Kikimora at her side. Sur, Diva's deer companion, had brought his entire herd, and they formed a protective circle around the mourners. The energy in the globes between the antlers of the six-winged deer sparked purple with hues of yellow, displaying both their anger and sorrow.

In the water, the green-haired Rusalki had gathered. Garments of finely woven silver nets shimmered throughout the water for as far as Theo could see. The Rusalki's ghastly queen, Vodna, floated in front of the group. Her eight tentacles, embedded with emeralds, dipped in and out of the water, as if she were impatient to be away. With his dragon hearing, Theo listened to the gems rattling, and he shivered, remembering his encounter with her. He still regretted having to give her a kaval that had belonged to Zunitza, even though he'd learned that it had only been a temporary gift for his mother. His Rusalka friend, Ruslana, and her sister, Dimana, floated on either side of the Queen of the Water Kingdom.

A flutter of wings drew Theo's attention back to Diva. The magpie Boo hopped close to his fallen friend and laid a single white blossom over her heart. Smil, the magical, healing flower that grew only in Zmeykovo. It was the harvesting of this flower that had originally brought Boo to Zmeykovo, back when he was only a fledgling. Now, the magpie had become the Samodivi's trusted messenger.

"Zmey." Sava, the eldest of Diva's sisters, addressed her king. "All may not be lost."

The dragon king squeezed Diva's lifeless hand and placed it over his heart before standing. A spark of hope lit his mournful eyes.

"We know of a sacred ritual to revive the spirit." Sava looked down at Diva, and then back to Zmey. "Even now, I can feel my sister's presence hovering around her body. However, we mustn't delay, for her essence weakens even as we speak."

Zmey clasped the nymph's hands. "Do what you must. Please bring my daughter back."

"We'll do our best." Sava bowed her head, and then raised her voice to those gathered. "It is time. Gather closer."

Beneath the sliver of a moon, the Samodivi drew near. Their bare feet barely seemed to touch the sand as they formed three circles around Diva and the willow. Behind them, Sitara and Drakus joined the Kukeri to create another circle.

Pavel reclaimed his seat beside Diva, and Theo glanced at his father, who nodded. Theo sat at his sister's other side, while Zmey took his place by Diva's feet. Theo and Pavel each took one of

Diva's hands. Boo nudged Theo, as if wanting to offer comfort, but the magpie remained silent. Grateful for Boo's presence, Theo stroked the bird's feathers with his free hand.

Golden droplets from Samodivi Lake continued to sprinkle those gathered. Theo squeezed his eyes close for a brief moment, thinking about how Diva had once administered the lake's water to heal forest animals. Would the life-giving liquid now achieve the same benefit for her? Could it bring her back from death with the assistance of the Samodivi ritual?

So much about the magical land of Zmeykovo remained a mystery. This ritual would have been something Diva would have explained to him if she hadn't been unresponsive and at death's door. He tightened his grip on her cold hand as thoughts of the many things she'd taught him about her homeland raced through his mind. Only a little more than a year ago, she'd befriended him and assisted with his quest to save his human sister, Nia. Back then, when he'd landed for the first time in this strange, mystical land, he'd been a scrawny boy, unsure of himself.

Pleading with his eyes, he begged Sava in his mind. *"Please, let this work. Bring back my friend, my sister."*

A hush fell over the shoreline as Sava raised her arms toward the moon. The breeze stilled, and the lake calmed, ceasing to scatter its golden dew. Within the surrounding forest, animals halted their nocturnal scampering. Not a twig cracked. Not a bush rustled. Not a creature made a sound. Glowing pairs of eyes blinked amid the trees. Waiting. Listening. Watching.

A chill swept over Theo, certain he'd felt fingertips grasping his shoulder. Across from him, Pavel shivered. He raised red-rimmed eyes toward Theo. *"Did you feel that?"*

Theo gave his best friend a small nod. Ever since Theo had entered Pavel's mind to save him from the song of Sirin, one of the birds of paradise, the two boys had been able to communicate with their thoughts, the way Theo and Diva talked to one another.

"Was that you, Diva?" Theo sent the question to her.

His heart sank. No affirmation or words of encouragement penetrated his mind. Was Diva's spirit truly hovering the way Sava had claimed?

Theo lifted his head to see what Sava was doing. The Samodiva swayed slightly as she continued to hold her hands aloft. Then she began to hum. Low at first, the melody sent vibrations through Theo's body. As the tune intensified, the air thickened, becoming heavy with a hazy golden moisture, as if Sava was pulling the lake water toward her. She glided her hands through the air, and the mist swirled, undulating like a snake. Long tendrils twisted around each other over Diva like a hypnotic circle, growing smaller as they reached toward infinity.

Sava added words to her song, the melody reaching into Theo's soul. "Bendis, Goddess of the Moon, hear our melancholy tune. Look down upon our sorrow. Come to us before the morrow. We beseech your aid. Let not our beloved fade."

One at a time, the other Samodivi joined their voices with Sava's. The Kukeri began to dance in place. It wasn't the frenetic dance filled with hopping and flailing limbs that they performed to chase away evil, but rather the movements were slow and mellow. Bells around the men's waists banged against each other, a low clanging, adding a muted background to the nymphs' melodious voices. In the water, the enchanting, hypnotizing voices of the Rusalki intensified to mix with the other sounds.

The moon rose higher, growing fuller as it ascended. Twinkling stars brightened as they danced across the heavens.

The Samodivi joined hands and performed a slow horo, a circular dance, around Diva and the willow. Each circle of participants moved in the opposite direction to the one in front of it. The tree's branches joined in and rustled and swayed in time to the nymphs' fluid, graceful movements.

On the ground, the golden mist spread out and gently covered Diva. Electrical pinpricks crept up Theo's fingers where he held her hand. When he looked toward Pavel, his friend nodded, acknowledging he'd experienced the same feeling. Boo squeezed himself closer to both Diva and Theo, as if being ready to protect his friends. Zmey, meanwhile, stood immobile, his hands clasped in front, as he continued to gaze at his daughter's pale face.

When the moon was nearly full, the Samodivi's dance sped up, and their voices rang louder. The Kukeri's movements became more chaotic, their bells swinging and clanging, this time loud enough to chase away any evil intruder. The lake churned with the tumultuous activity of the Rusalki. Even the willow branches thrashed about, and the leaves twisted and turned as if disturbed by a whirlwind. Within the forest, creatures growled, hissed, and squealed. The animals' glowing eyes flashed from one location to another, barely remaining still.

Boo pressed even closer to Theo, who gripped Diva's hand harder, not knowing if she'd somehow float away toward the moon. Across from him, Pavel had grabbed hold of Diva with both hands. His mouth was pressed into a tight line, his face had reddened, and his brow was creased. Zmey, too, appeared anxious, as he twisted his hands.

The dancing became a whir. The nymphs' and Rusalki's voices merged into a melodic, hypnotic hum, like a swarm of bees. Theo's heart raced with the commotion. The ritual appeared to be reaching its peak as the moon became full.

When the moon's light brightened the sky, all dancing and chanting ceased at once, as if choreographed. Each Samodiva thrust her hands skyward with the last ring of the bells. The women lifted their faces, their lips silently moving, as if communing with the spirit of the moon.

Sava raised her hands and face along with the others and shouted once more, "Bendis, Goddess of the Moon, hear our melancholy tune. Look down upon our sorrow. Come to us before the morrow. We beseech your aid. Let not our beloved fade."

A beam of moonlight shot down, engulfing the willow with a silver glow. Branches rustled, and leaves dropped one by one. Each turned into a white butterfly that surrounded Diva like a tight cocoon. Specs of the golden mist peeked through as the insects hovered above their charge.

Now silent, the Samodivi and Kukeri tightened their circles around Diva, while the Rusalki gathered close to the shore. Nocturnal and daytime creatures swarmed from the forest, wending their way to the gathering, where they mingled among the Samodivi and Kukeri. Birds flew above, chirping, peeping, cawing, and hooting. Grunts, growls, hisses, and other sounds came from beasts, some of which Theo had never seen before.

Above them, the wind rustled, and the creatures ceased their noises as one.

Theo glanced toward the canopy of the starlit sky. Two pure white winged deer with shimmering, ethereal wings pulled a silver carriage. Intricate designs of serpents made from sapphires adorned the vehicle. Inside, two priestesses, dressed in flowing white robes, flanked the goddess Bendis. Her image glowed like the moon she ruled.

As she passed overhead, the goddess scattered sparkling silver dust. It swirled in circles, speckling the butterflies. They shook their wings, sprinkling the dust over every part of Diva. Silver sparkled within the golden mist.

Theo held his breath as the mist began to dissipate. *"Diva, come back to us,"* he thought to her.

Silence reigned on the beach and throughout the forest. Theo couldn't hear anyone breathing, not even with his dragon senses, as everyone waited for a sign of life from Diva. Her pale face remained translucent, and the hand Theo held had warmed only because of his tight grip.

Sniffling, Pavel gently tapped Diva on the cheek. "Come on. Wake up. We need you."

A moment later, Zmey dropped to his knees next to Theo. "My daughter, please return to us." The dragon king kissed Diva on the forehead and stroked his fingers over her braids.

Diva's sisters murmured chants, reaching up once again to the now vacant sky, pleading toward the moon for Diva's protection and cure. The magpie Boo laid his head against his fallen friend's side. Jega, Sitara, and Drakus had somehow made their way through the crowded space, and they, too, lowered themselves to the sand around Diva. Theo's friends all placed their hands on the unmoving girl as if infusing their own magical powers into her.

Everyone was pressed so close Theo almost missed it. A soft *thump*. He drew in a quick breath, wondering if it had come from one of the animals or his friends who surrounded Diva. He shook his head to clear his mind and focused all his dragon senses on Diva, blocking out everyone else.

He waited. One. Two. Three. *Thump.* A heartbeat. Still soft. Still weak. But a sign of returning life.

Zmey must have heard it, too, because he rose. Everyone quieted when he cleared his throat.

"Diva." His voice cracked. "My daughter … The ritual has merged her spirit with her body."

"Yay, Diva." Pavel wrapped his arms around her. A weak smile lit his exhausted face.

"The power of the moon was not enough to restore her fully," Zmey continued. "The Golden Apple is the only certain cure."

"What about Mom's robe and belt?" Theo asked. "You said they have healing power."

Zmey nodded. "They do. A Samodiva's clothing, especially that of the queen, is quite powerful. However, if the Moon Goddess Ritual couldn't completely revive Diva, it's unlikely your mother's robe will have enough power either."

Jega rose and bowed to Zmey. "My brothers and I will assist you in retrieving the Golden Apple in any way you require."

"As will I and the Samodivi," Sava added.

The Rusalki remained quiet and silently slipped away, back to their underwater world. Just like before. Theo recalled how their beach had remained untouched during Lamia's rampage through Zmeykovo. Whether they had some hidden agreement with the beastly dragon, or whether they preferred to remain neutral, he wasn't certain. At least they had attended the ritual and provided Diva what support they could.

"I need …" Zmey looked at his unresponsive daughter. "I need someone to care for Diva."

Ula stepped forward. "I shall stay with her. I'll take her back to her room in our fortress."

"Thank you." Zmey lowered his head to Ula. "My daughter couldn't ask for anyone with a kinder heart."

Theo was torn. He wanted to go with his father, but he didn't want to leave Diva. Pavel hadn't spoken, but, of course, he would remain with their friend, so Theo made up his mind. He could do both.

"Father, I will accompany Ula. I can be her eyes and ears until we get to the fortress. When everything's settled there, I'll return to the castle to help with battle preparations."

Zmey nodded. "Well spoken, my son. Guard them well."

In moments, the area had cleared of warriors and forest animals alike, leaving Theo, Pavel, Ula, and Diva alone. Boo had remained as well. Sur, Shar, Whirl, and Ula's deer stood by, ready to transport everyone back to the fortress. As Ula mounted her deer, she cradled Diva in her arms.

"You ready, Pavel?" Theo asked.

His friend nodded and climbed onto Whirl, stroking the animal's neck. "Let's bring Diva home."

Theo wrapped his arms around Shar, feeling the comfort of the deer's beating heart. Soon, he hoped, Diva's would beat as strongly. He mounted the deer, and took one last look around, wanting to ensure no dangers lurked to follow them. As he scanned the forest, he stopped and stared at a gap between two towering oaks.

There stood a creature no higher than a tree stump. He resembled a man, but with branches and leaves sticking out all over him. The being's green glowing eyes stared at Theo before it disappeared into the darkness of the forest.

Chapter 2
The Search Begins

JULY 13

THE ROSY GLOW of the sun had crept over the horizon by the time Theo and his companions reached the fortress. Inside, Ula placed Diva upon a small bed that lay within a pale green tent. Diva's room hadn't changed since the time she had brought Theo here his first day in Zmeykovo. Books lay everywhere. On shelves by a fireplace, next to the bed, and littered all across the floor. Shadows and a soft amber glow flittered across them now from candles Ula had lit.

Theo recalled how terrified he'd been of Diva that day after she told him she was a Samodiva. She'd been indignant with him for fearing her more than he had the Harpy who attacked him. Despite feeling insulted, Diva had tended to his wounds with one of her many salves. The healing effects had been immediate. She'd also given him nourishment and told him to rest while she went out to care for the forest animals. As he gazed at Diva now, looking so fragile on her bed, he vowed that it was his turn to take care of her.

Ula left momentarily and returned with a fresh wreath of bay leaves and other herbs. She arranged the latter in a circle around Diva and placed the wreath on her head. "She has such a tenuous hold on life. I feel her spirit fading in and out. I don't know if she'll survive long enough for Zmey to retrieve the Golden Apple, let alone make it through the rest of today."

"We can't let her die." Pavel sat on the edge of the bed, holding Diva's hand. "But what can we do?"

"I'll find a way." Theo paced the room. "Maybe if I go to Kaleto Fortress alone, I can sneak in and find where Magda took my mother's robe and belt."

"Do you think she went back there?" Pavel asked. "Lamia was furious Magda had given her a fake apple. The beastly dragon called Magda a traitor and tried to kill her."

"I don't know." Theo ran his fingers through his hair. "She might have brought Lamia the real apple this time, hoping to be forgiven."

"That doesn't sound like something Magda would do," Ula said. "Once someone scorns her, or she even *thinks* they've done so, Magda seeks revenge. It's more likely she would hide somewhere while she plots."

Theo thought about his conversations with Magda. His aunt had shown such disdain for so many people. She made others out to be in the wrong, or she purposely tried to force wedges between people, casting doubt while she laid her plans.

"I'll track her down," he said. "I'll find out what she did with the Golden Apple, and I'll force her to tell me where my mother's robe and belt are. Ula, do you have any idea where Magda might hide?"

Ula steeled her face, her eyes growing hard. "I was never close to her. Magda was so off-putting, always feeling the victim, even though she brought on all her troubles. Zunitza was the only one who wanted to make Magda happy. She did everything for that beast, and look at how Magda repaid her. Can you communicate with Zunitza? She would be the only one who might know where to find Magda."

Theo shook his head. "No. My mother's been quiet. I sense her, but I think she's exhausted herself again by staying with Zmey while he was ill. Since she can't communicate with me, I'll go to her."

Pavel raised his head. "To the Forest of Souls?"

"Yes."

"Do you …?" Pavel looked at Diva again. "Do you want me to come with you?"

"I'd love your company." Theo paused. "But I think Ula needs you here more. What if one of you has to get supplies or … or anything? You can't leave Diva alone."

Ula nodded. "I'd appreciate it if you stayed, if you don't mind."

"Yes, of course, I'll stay. But what about Theo? Shouldn't someone go with him?"

Boo poked his head out from behind books, a seed dropping from his beak. "I'll go. The Samodivi don't need me right now. I can be Theo's messenger."

"Thank you, Boo," Pavel said.

Theo opened his eyes wide. "You understood him this time? You didn't hear *waak, waak* like you usually do?"

Pavel opened his mouth like a guppy. "I did understand him. I didn't even think that it was odd not to hear that obnoxious noise."

Boo tossed his head from side to side. "It's not obnoxious."

Theo laughed, glad for a bit of normalcy. "It must be because of our new connection. You seem to have gained some of my dragon abilities, Pavel. Maybe you can try to fly sometime."

Pavel shook his head and glanced back at Diva. "The only superpower I want right now is to help Diva get well."

"Me, too." Theo looked at her lying there, unmoving. "I'm leaving now. Take good care of my sister while I'm gone."

Ula gave Theo a hug. "You're now a sort-of brother to me. May Bendis watch over you and Boo and bring you back soon."

Theo thanked her and left with the magpie. Outside, he surveyed the fortress. It had been renovated from the ruins Lamia had inflicted upon the Samodivi residence. The rickety, burned boards had been removed and new ones added, and the fallen stones from the watchtower had been replaced. The fortress remained a ghost town at the moment, though, since the nymphs were strategizing with Zmey. Even so, signs of inhabitance were scattered around the courtyard. Flowers blossomed in gardens, and Theo breathed in their fragrant scents. Torches blazed in polished copper brackets. He ran his fingers along the engraving of a crescent moon over a sun on one of them.

"This will be like our first adventure, Boo. Just you and me."

"I've missed our time together." Boo pecked at a bug on Theo's sneakers.

"We were both so young and unaware of the dangers." Theo sighed. "At least this time, we know more about Zmeykovo, and now I can understand you."

"You did a good job of figuring everything out. We've both grown so much."

"I guess it's time to fly."

Theo stretched and willed himself to change into dragon form. In a matter of minutes, powerful wings emerged, his arms and legs became strong anchors, and his entire body expanded. The transformation felt more natural each time as Theo learned to master his gift.

After Boo hopped on, Theo unfurled his red wings and took to the sky. It would be good to see his mother again and not just speak with her in his mind.

The land below felt peaceful for once. Was it because Lamia had what she wanted? What if Ula was wrong and Magda had returned to Kaleto Fortress and given the beastly dragon the Golden Apple? Magda might put aside her resentment and give the powerful fruit to Lamia in exchange for becoming the queen of the Samodivi, a role Magda thought should have always been hers.

If that's true, Lamia's probably preparing another elaborate ceremony right now.

It was likely to be one that would make the world bow down and acknowledge her. She pursued power instead of the love Theo was certain she truly craved. She must have been good once, since Zmey had so much love in his heart for his sister. Or at least he had until Lamia murdered Diva. Hurting a parent's child was a line no one should cross without expecting to pay the consequences.

Diva, I'm going to save you. I'm sure of it.

Zmey wasn't the only one Lamia should fear. Theo had become a menacing foe.

As he flew over various landmarks, he thought back to the many adventures and dangers he'd experienced in Zmeykovo. Below him was Rodina Forest. He and Diva had trekked through it to get to the temple of the goddess Bendis. Along the way, they'd encountered terrifying gnats that could crawl inside a person and eat them from the inside out.

Cherna Mountain now lay ahead of him. Theo recalled sloshing his way through the putrid-smelling tunnel to sneak into the castle. There, they'd discovered Zandan, the prison. He shuddered at the memory of the torture devices and the emaciated condition of the prisoners.

South of him was the Cold Marsh, where Jabalaka had been hiding. Kikimora, Lord Vodnik, and Sly, the water king's adopted son, all lived there, too. Up ahead, he passed Vida Fortress, where the evil nymphs called Youdi lived. Beyond that lay Kadin Bridge, where he'd met Struma, the ghost of a woman sacrificed to be the protector of the bridge. It was here that they'd also encountered Bor Stobor, the Karakonjul, a half-man, half-horse creature.

The towering megaliths, marking where the Kukeri lived, rose in front of Theo. The first time he'd met Mraz, Zima, and Jega, Theo had thought the men were going to eat him and Pavel. Instead, they'd turned out to be allies.

Diva had been there for almost every challenge he'd faced. She befriended him, guided him, and helped him grow and believe in himself. But, the time to reminisce had ended. At last, Theo had reached the Forest of Souls. From this height, the glowing spheres within the forest looked like twinkling stars.

Theo dove toward the trees and landed outside the forest. He breathed in the incense aroma the trees emitted from their bark, blackened and cracked from their ancient age. Leafless branches cradled spheres, in which the souls of Zmeykovo's ancestors resided. The first time Theo was here, he'd learned that the spheres used their essence to feed the trees. When he had touched a tree's bark, he'd felt heat flowing through it like sap. The relationship between the trees and spheres enabled the forest to survive during Lamia's destruction of much of Zmeykovo.

Theo gazed at the forest in amazement. So many spheres cast golden light everywhere he looked. He wondered if Zima was here, or if his spirit had completely returned to nature when he died. Theo wished he had time to search for his fallen friend, but the tug of Zunitza's sphere beckoned Theo toward the center of the forest.

He shifted back to boy form with ease and glanced at the magpie, who pecked at bugs on the ground. "You ready, Boo?"

"Ready, ready." Boo flew onto a branch. "Lead the way."

As Theo wound his way among the trees, a feeling of peace enveloped him. Zmeykovo's ancestors were sending him their blessings, calling him the young prince. Their whispered words of encouragement and faith in him eased the pain he'd experienced about the deception around the Golden Apple.

Theo had never carried the real one with him back from the Znahar Tree, where he'd harvested the fruit. Zmey had confessed to Theo that Kosara gave him a decoy to protect the real apple from their enemies. At the time, Theo believed the deception was really a test of his own trustworthiness. He thought Zmey, the priestess Kosara, and the Colobari had believed Theo would be overcome by the apple's power.

He let go of the betrayal and acknowledged that the plan had been the right one. As much as Theo had wanted to bring the apple back to the castle, he realized now that he hadn't failed. He'd allowed the apple to make it back safely, even if Magda had later stolen the magical fruit, despite everyone's efforts to keep it safe.

By the time he reached the tree that held his mother's sphere, Theo felt a heavy weight lift from his heart. He could focus on finding a way to save Diva, without thoughts of betrayal and deception occupying his mind.

The familiar scent of honeysuckle wafted from the tree as the golden sphere slowly began to spin. While it rotated, misty colors within rippled, light violet and rose intermingling. Little by little, the colors faded, and the sphere ceased spinning. The person Theo had longed to see emerged. His mother's ethereal face, surrounded by her fiery red hair like his own, filled his heart with love.

"Mother." He touched the cold, smooth sphere.

She reached toward him from inside, mirroring his gesture. "My beloved son."

More pain melted away as Zunitza infused him with her thoughts and emotions. Theo felt his anger toward Magda and Lamia flow from his body and dissipate into the air. Sorrow for what the women had become filled the empty space. If his parents could continue to love their siblings despite all the treachery both his aunts had inflicted, then Theo could as well. That didn't mean he wouldn't destroy them if it became necessary, but he wouldn't let hate rule his actions.

"Mother, I have to save Diva. Magda …"

Unable to say the words, he sent Zunitza his own thoughts of everything that had happened, all of Magda's betrayals. Her attempt to befriend him, when all she wanted was access to the Golden Apple. Her confession that she herself should have been queen of the Samodivi. Her accusations against Diva, trying to frame her for stealing Zunitza's belt and seeking power.

He concluded by choking out, "She stole everything that could save Diva: the Golden Apple and your robe and belt. And I caught her wearing your wedding dress once. She said it was because she missed you, but now we know that was a lie. She wanted to *be* you, to have everything that you had."

Zunitza wiped away moisture from the side of her eyes. "I tried so hard to make her see that she was special, that she had her own unique abilities. What she had was never enough for her. She put on airs and disdained everyone she thought was beneath her."

"We're running out of time to save Diva." Theo paced near the tree. "I have to find Magda, but I don't know where to look. You must remember places she liked to go. Somewhere she might be hiding now."

His mother rubbed her chin. "I can think of a couple of places. Both were near the tip of the dragon's tail."

"Dragon's tail?" Theo recalled the first time he'd seen a map of Zmeykovo. Its shape had reminded him of a dragon, too. He hadn't considered that others who lived here would call it that as well. Sometimes, people didn't see their homeland the way others perceived it.

Zunitza smiled. "That's what we called it, back when Magda was friendlier toward me. It's the stretch of land on the eastern side of Zmeykovo that overlooks Rusalki Bay."

"There's a lot of land out that way," Theo said. "What are the places you remember?"

"One is a glen at the farthest end of the dragon tail. We built a secret hideaway there, surrounded by the forest." Zunitza's face glowed as if remembering good times. "We could smell the sea air and hear the Rusalki singing. We liked to sneak to the edge of the cliff and spy on their activities."

As she spoke, her voice began to fade, and her image grew blurry.

Theo placed his face closer to the sphere. "Mother, don't leave me!"

"Getting weaker. Must hurry," she whispered, her words tumbling from her lips. "The other place is an outcropping of rocks that jut up through a dense forest. It's near the village of Surnitza."

"Anywhere else?"

Zunitza shook her head. Her next words were barely audible. "Those were the only places that were ours. Places we liked to escape to."

The sphere began to grow misty again, violet and rose hues intertwining.

"I must leave you now." Her words were the softest whisper. "My energy fades."

"Thank you, Mother." Tears riddled his eyes as he placed his hand back onto the cool sphere. "Rest now. I'll try to connect with you when I'm there if I find her."

Zunitza's image faded, along with the scent of honeysuckle. His mother was gone, resting. She'd used up so much energy being with Zmey during his illness. Theo was thankful she had been able to give him a couple locations to search. He was certain he would find the treacherous Magda hiding in one of them. He just hoped she had the stolen items with her.

Chapter 3
Hideaways

ALTHOUGH THEO HAD TRAVELED to Rusalki Bay before, the dragon's tail was a part of Zmeykovo he had yet to explore. The stretch of land separated the eastern side of the bay from the more turbulent sea surrounding the island. He wished Diva and Pavel were here for the adventure. Theo missed his sister's practical advice and his best friend's inventions, even if they didn't always work as expected.

Boo let out a squawk, as if reading Theo's thoughts.

"Yes, Boo, I'm thankful you're with me. I wish all my friends could be here."

That seemed to calm the bird. He nestled into Theo's neck, just like old times when the then-baby magpie liked to ride on Theo's shoulders.

From this height, just below the clouds, the land looked peaceful. Forests abutted craggy ledges at the water's edge, and huts dotted the terrain. A perfect place for Magda to hide.

Huts became more frequent up ahead, and soon Theo flew over a larger village that must be Surnitza. Residents scurried around like busy ants. The effects of war weren't evident to Theo from so high in the sky, but he was sure those below hadn't remained unscathed by Lamia and Zlo's thirst for power and immortality.

Not far past the village, pillars rose from the top of a hill. They poked their heads above the dense forest like curious prairie dogs, checking their surroundings. As Theo flew closer, he observed that the heads on the rock formations resembled snakes. The entire configuration, in fact, staggered across the hillside like a slithering snake.

So many pillars! And likely more smaller ones lay hidden among the trees.

"How are we going to search them all?" Theo thought to Boo.

"One at a time," the magpie squawked back.

Theo wanted to roll his eyes. Instead, he enhanced his dragon vision to look for movement within the visible pillars. If his mother and Magda liked to observe the world, they would have found a place in the tallest ones, perhaps a carved-out area where they could sit and peer at everything going on around them.

Something black darted around one of the snake heads and disappeared.

"There!" he thought to Boo. *"Did you see that?"*

"Yes, yes," Boo shouted near Theo's ear. "That must be Magda. Hurry and get her."

Theo tucked in his wings and dove toward the pillar. As he got closer, more and more black shapes appeared, zipping in and out of crevices in the rocks.

Snakes. Hundreds and hundreds of the creatures swarmed the rock face. Not only the one where he thought Magda hid, but the others.

"It's a city of snakes!"

He found it difficult to believe Magda would be in there. To be certain, he tuned in his dragon hearing as he circled the structures. No breathing. Only the hissing of the creatures that now claimed one of his mother's jaunts. She'd been gone so long the place had become overridden with the beasts.

Theo reversed course and took to the clouds. He wasn't going to find his aunt among the snakes. It was time to search for the other hiding place. He flew toward the tip of the dragon's tail.

On the bay side, stretches of glistening white sand stretched along the coastline. That sand had proven to be scorching, a way for the Rusalki to deter trespassers. Pavel hadn't heeded Diva's warning. He'd taken off his shoes and rushed toward the water. Just as quickly, he'd screeched and hurried back to the grass. Theo hadn't believed Pavel that it could be that hot and touched it with his fingertips. It had seared them. Unlike Pavel, Theo had acted macho, pretending the sand hadn't burned.

Diva had proven her point that they should listen to her. Despite her warnings, both he and Pavel continued to make bad decisions in their travels. They didn't believe that Zmeykovo could hold all the dangers Diva spoke about. But with each trial, they learned that it did. This wasn't the non-magical human world, after all. Their own world held other kinds of dangers, but ones Theo knew how to avoid.

That felt like ages ago, when they hadn't had to make adult decisions. And when Diva had been alive. Theo sighed. It was too late to return to childhood innocence. Their Zmeykovo experiences had ensured that. But Theo was determined to make sure all three of them could have more adventures, safe ones, in this magical land.

"*Boo*," he thought to the magpie. "*You've been the Samodivi's messenger. Have you ever come across something that might be the secret hideaway my mother spoke about?*"

"Maybe, maybe." Boo peeked over Theo's shoulder. "Fly to the tip. I can show you the way from there."

Theo's mother had said the hideaway she and Magda had frequented lay near a glen. The forest's dense canopy of towering trees, however, sheltered any open spaces within their midst. Theo circled lower and lower until he found an area among the trees that was wide enough for him to land. He unfurled his wings to slow his descent.

As his claws sank into a thick carpet of moss, the ground trembled. The force of his landing hurled mossy fragments into the air, and a fresh, earthy scent rose to greet him. Otherwise, his arrival seemed unwelcomed. The forest had stilled. Theo sensed the fear of the creatures hiding within their sanctuary, as if no being had ever intruded here before—at least not something as powerful as a dragon. He wanted to allay their panic, but as he touched them with his mind, their bodies quivered, and their hearts raced.

He hurried to shift into boy form, and the forest seemed to release a breath of relief. Sounds resumed as animals skittered through the undergrowth and birds flittered from branch to branch, tweeting happy tunes. Even the leaves resumed their soft rustling.

Having calmed the creatures' fears, Theo took in the splendor of the glen. Nature and magic intertwined within the tranquility of the secluded realm. Sunlight filtering through the thick foliage speckled every surface: the moss, the leaves, the brook that babbled nearby. On the ground, he could now tell that this was an ancient forest. Lichens and moss covered the gnarled oaks and maples, while tall pines, devoid of lower branches, reached for the sky.

Amid it all, the air tingled with an as-yet-to-be-discovered enchantment. Something otherworldly lived here as well. Theo felt it prying into his being, probing to see if he was friend or foe—not so much of the creature itself, but of the forest and animals. Whatever it was that lived here was the guardian of these woods and would not tolerate harm coming to its charges.

Let it come to me. I will not seek it out. Nor will I disrupt its home if I can avoid it.

He stood for a moment, breathing in the fresh, pine-scented air and listening to the murmuring of the brook. If only all of Zmeykovo could be so serene.

"Theo." Boo tapped his beak on Theo's leg. "If we follow the brook, we'll find the hiding place."

Theo drew in another long breath, held it, then released it slowly. His gut told him it wouldn't be long before the feeling of peace evaporated, and he wanted to savor it a while longer.

He followed Boo as the magpie flew from branch to branch, swooping down from time to time to peck at a fat bug sunning on a rock. The forest along both sides of the brook grew denser the farther they traveled.

All the while, Theo sensed the mystical being following them, just out of sight. Even Theo's enhanced dragon senses couldn't pick up sight or smell of the forest guardian, as if it had turned invisible or masked its presence by some sort of camouflage.

Theo's tingling skin, however, made him aware it was there, ready to pounce if Theo made one wrong move.

He stopped to listen and scan the forest from time to time, not wanting the being to catch him unaware. The trees, or a particular one, an ancient, moss-covered fir, seemed to be in sight every time he looked. This tree resembled a witch with long, tangled hair. The branches looked like skinny, interlaced fingers, that wanted to unclench and grab Theo. He approached it once when Boo had discovered a hoard of bugs inside a rotted log. Theo walked around the tree, touched it, sent his dragons senses to probe it. It truly was a tree, not a strange being. And yet … something about it was off.

After following the brook for a while, they came to a triangle mark resembling a slingshot.

"The cabin's this way." Boo flew on ahead, stopping a short distance away on an oak twisted around a maple. Another of the triangular marks lay at the base of the entwined trees.

Onward they trudged through the forest, following the marks up an overgrown incline. The sound of the sea crashing against cliffs mingled with forest noises. Soon rocky ground replaced undergrowth.

"Almost there." Boo rested on another strange tree, this one three oaks twisted around each other as if someone had been plying rope.

As they continued upward, the trees thinned, and the sea became louder. A moment later, Theo stepped out into an open area. A rickety hut there looked as if it had been built from the hollow of a massive old tree. Patches of *Amanita muscaria* grew around the tree-hut, which stood close to the cliff edge, granting him a spectacular view of both Rusalki Bay and the sea. The hut blended into the scenery, with trees growing right up to it, concealing it from aerial view. A perfect place to hide from a dragon flying overhead.

Theo glanced around, searching for the strange tree that had continued to follow him. He sighed with relief that all the trees here appeared normal.

"Thank you, Boo. How did you ever discover this place?"

"I followed Lesnik's marks."

Theo raised an eyebrow. "Lesnik? Like Kikimora's husband? He made those?"

"Yes, yes." Boo hopped closer to the hut. "This is where he hides out."

Theo wanted to know more about the being who had married Kiki and then deserted her, but at the moment, it was more urgent to find Magda. "Let's hope my aunt's here instead."

He walked toward the lopsided door, which looked as if it hadn't moved in ages. Cobwebs filled in the cracks, and moss had grown along the jamb. Thinking it would stick, Theo pushed hard against the door. It swung inside, slamming against the wall, without making a creak or scraping against the wooden floors inside.

"Someone's been here recently," he said to Boo.

The single room was free of dust, and everything appeared tidy. Empty bottles in descending height lined a bookcase. In the corner, a bed had been made with military precision, not a wrinkle in sight. Wood stacked by the fireplace was evenly spaced, the ends lining up. Chairs had been spaced equidistant around a table. Not a thing was out of place.

"If this is where Lesnik lives," Theo said, "I can understand why he had trouble staying with Kiki."

The chicken lady made chaos out of everything she touched, especially when she tried to clean her home. Someone who left everything in order, like in this hut, must have been driven crazy with trying to keep on top of Kiki's messes.

"Yes, yes. I agree." Boo hopped around the room, poking his head into corners and looking under furniture. "It doesn't appear your aunt has been here."

Theo sighed and ran his fingers through his hair. "You're right. I don't know where else to look. My mother thought this was the best place to find Magda."

A loud, cackling laugh came from beyond the door. "You'll never find me."

"That was her!" Theo ran outside.

A tall, slim figure wearing black darted into the forest.

"Boo, we have to stop her." Theo ran in pursuit of his aunt.

"Wait, Theo." Boo zipped out of the hut. "I don't think—"

More hysterical laughter erupted from behind a towering oak, drowning out Boo's words.

Theo ran from tree to tree. Each time he thought he could seize the mysterious figure in black, she seemed to melt into the air. Mere moments later, her laughter came from a different location.

"Theo, stop." Boo hovered in front of Theo. "I don't think that's your aunt."

Exhausted, Theo bent over, his hands on his knees to catch his breath.

"Who else could it be?" He raised his head and took deep gulping breaths of air.

He stepped back. That mossy-covered fir tree was right in front of him. "Am I hallucinating?"

"No, you're not." Boo landed on a branch on the fir and started pecking the bark. The tree appeared to shrink back.

Theo opened his eyes wide. "Did the tree just … flinch?"

"Yes, I tried to tell you it wasn't your aunt."

"Then who … what is it?"

"Lesnik himself. I'll show you." Boo ruffled his feathers and stood with his beak held high. "Lesnik, Forest Lord, come to us now, not as a gray wolf, not as a black raven, not as a flaming fir tree, but as a man."

Theo blinked, and the strange tree disappeared. In its place stood an old man with long, scraggly hair that he'd combed to the left side. His head was slightly pointed, and two goat horns protruded from it. His face was pallid like that of the Samodivi, only it looked rough like bark and was blue-tinged. A large wart on the man's face shifted around. His blazing green eyes were crossed and held a feral look as the creature stared back at Theo. A thick coat of hair covered him, from his beard to his arms, legs, and torso. And it was all green. Although hairy everywhere else, the man lacked eyebrows and eyelashes. He appeared to have grown out of the wood itself.

And his attire … He looked like a toddler who had dressed himself. The man wore his buttonless clothes backward, and unlike adults Theo knew in Selo, this man went beltless. Theo cringed when he observed the man's footwear. It must hurt Lesnik to walk since his bast boots occupied the wrong feet.

Laughter erupted from Lesnik. A horn tied to the creature's side swayed from side to side as he shook toward Theo a wooden club he gripped in his clawed hands. Lesnik seemed to be saying he'd beat Theo if he dared be rude or show the man disrespect in any way.

Being rude was the last thing on Theo's mind as dizziness overcame him. The man grew and shrank before Theo's eyes. At one moment, he was as tall as the tallest tree. The next instance, the man had shrunk to the size of a blade of grass. Sunlight danced around him as he changed form, yet he cast no shadow.

"Stop it." Theo placed his hands on the side of his head. "You're giving me a headache."

Boo pecked at the man's shin, and Lesnik settled for a height to match Theo's.

"Is it magic you seek, or do you wish to make a bargain with me?" Lesnik asked.

"Neither." Theo shook his head. "I came here to find Magda, my aunt. She has … something I need." Theo wasn't certain he could trust the old tree-man with the story. He had a look about him that said he would sell out to the highest bidder.

"Ah, so it's information you seek," Lesnik said. "Perhaps I can assist with that."

"Do you know where I can find her? It's really important that I get the things she … get some stuff back from her soon."

Lesnik's green eyes sparkled with fire. "Of course, I do, but I'll want something in return."

"Be careful, Theo." Boo hopped between the two of them. "Lesnik likes to play tricks and will get the best of you if you're not careful."

Theo snorted. "Sounds like Baba Yaga." He patted his sword. "I can take care of that kind of treachery with this."

"Now, don't be hasty." Lesnik took a step back into the shadows. "What I want is simple. My wife brews the most potent beer. I've gone dry with my long absence. Bring me a case full, and I'll tell you what you need to know."

"You'd be better off with an herbal tea."

"Tea is for gossip, beer is for … never mind. Just bring the beer and meet me in the Cold Marsh. I'll be with Lord Vodnik. One must drink with friends to make it more enjoyable." With a bow, Lesnik disappeared. "I'll be there in a wink and a kiss of the wind. Come join me soon."

"Maybe I'll bring you what you want," Theo mumbled to the air. "But not right away."

He didn't have time for this nonsense. Everyone wanted something in exchange for making Zmeykovo safe. Apparently, Theo had no other choice. He couldn't scour every place in Zmeykovo looking for Magda. He only hoped that he wouldn't be too late to save Diva.

Chapter 4
The Cold Marsh

THE DAY WAS HALF OVER by the time Theo arrived at the Cold Marsh. He'd wasted so much time … no, Lesnik had wasted Theo's time, chasing after the forest guardian. That creature cared more for his tricks and games than he did for Diva, even though she had the same goals as he did—protecting forest animals.

And Lord Vodnik! Theo had little if anything nice to say about that monster. He'd viciously murdered one of his wives—a human one he'd kidnapped no less. Not only his wife, but he'd also killed the child they'd had together, as well as enslaved children of other water creatures he'd deposed. He dared to call them his children, but he wasn't above torturing them. How someone like Lord Vodnik had been allowed to be a ruler in Zmeykovo still baffled Theo. Couldn't Zmey or someone else replace the beast?

But because no one had, Theo now needed to return to deal with that monster, along with put up with more of Lesnik's trickery. Theo refused to go first to Kikimora's home on the other side of the marsh to beg her for beer for her wayward husband. It was preferable to drag the forest guardian back to her and let her deal with Lesnik. Kiki was so lonely she'd probably be delighted to see her husband and give him all the beer he wanted.

If the two of them didn't give Theo the information he needed, he'd use his sword to convince them. The weapon had the power to injure Lord Zlo, so Theo was certain it could deal with the two selfish friends, who were forcing him to travel around Zmeykovo instead of helping him save Diva.

Theo landed with a *thud* on the outskirts of the marsh, by the river they'd traveled along when they'd gone to Kadin Bridge. He didn't dare get too close as a dragon. When he'd traveled here before with Diva, he had been in boy form, and he'd sunk into the muck. His much larger and heavier dragon form would likely get stuck permanently.

"Let's do this, Boo," Theo said when he'd shifted once more. "I suppose we'll need some kind of 'shiny' to attract Lord Vodnik's attention, since I'm not sure exactly where we'll find him this time. Do you have any ideas?"

"Magpies are good at finding shiny things." Boo flew off in search of a trinket.

Moments later, he returned with a tear-shaped belt buckle like the ones the Samodivi wore. This one was embellished with an island scene in the midst of a storm. The force of the wind bent trees, and waves rose high on all sides. Small rubies lay scattered around the edges of the buckle. Gaps in the design showed where some gems had gone missing. Theo wondered about the nymph who had lost it. Was she still alive? Or had she fought a battle here in the past and now rested in the Forest of Souls?

Either way, he believed she would be delighted for Theo to give the buckle to Lord Vodnik in order to save Diva.

"Thank you, Boo. This will be perfect."

Theo wiped off the slime as best he could on his pants leg. Every other time he'd been in the marsh, he'd come out coated with the gunk. He imagined today would be much the same.

"I guess any path will eventually lead us to where Lord Vodnik and Lesnik are." He ventured into the murky darkness, following a narrow path, carpeted with soft moss. "Sly, are you here? Can you lead us to your father?" Theo said the last word with a sneer.

He didn't expect the young Vodnik, who looked like an old man, to respond. He was likely either taking care of Lord Vodnik's cattle or in the hidden castle library, helping their mutual friend, Jabalaka. Any of the other Vodni would want the buckle to help, so Theo kept his calls to Sly.

Boo echoed Theo's words. Although Theo heard words, he imagined that to the beings living in the marsh, Boo sounded more like "*Waak, waak.*"

They traveled along a path, calling, stopping to listen, then continuing on through the putrid-smelling marsh. Broken limbs on moss-covered trees creaked and groaned as they passed. No one answered them, but plenty of creatures croaked, belched, and peeped all around. Twin pairs of eyes followed them, blinking like faulty lights.

Theo stopped, clenched his fists, and screamed, "This is ridiculous. Lord Vodnik, we don't have time to play games. Tell us where to find you!"

A mossy tree creaked and leaned to its side. Theo hurried out of its path to avoid getting splashed when it fell into the nasty water.

Only the tree didn't topple. It slunk away.

"You and your stupid games." He chased after the retreating tree for another game of catch-me-if-you-can with Lesnik.

Boo shot after the tree, pecking it and ripping off mossy strands. The tree-Lesnik twitched its branches, but even so, he didn't stop. He zig-zagged his way through the marsh. Sometimes, he was a dot in the distance. Other times, he was within inches of Theo's grasp.

After what felt like a long pursuit, Theo stopped running and screamed once more, "I've had enough! Bring me to Lord Vodnik now, or I'll find another way to save my sister."

Boo squawked, "I walked. I found. I lost."

Theo was about to ask what that meant when the tree-Lesnik transformed into his man appearance and said, "You figured it out!"

In a blink of an eye, he disappeared once more, and mist replaced the location where he had been standing. Theo's teeth chattered as the temperature dropped to freezing. A sudden silence fell over the marsh moments before a gale ripped through the trees, whirling the ever-thickening mist around Theo and Boo. Trees groaned as they cracked and splashed into the marsh.

The mist became so dense it obscured Theo's vision. He waved his hands in front of himself, but he still couldn't walk forward or backward for fear of stepping into the sulfuric-smelling water. Under the strain of the winds, the mossy path beneath him rippled and swayed like a living creature. Theo stumbled, reaching out for anything to hold onto to keep his balance. Only air met his grasp, and he fell face-first into the marsh-soaked path.

"Boo, where are you?" he called as he wiped the muck from his face.

"Keep talking, and I'll come to you," the magpie replied.

"What happened to Lesnik? I can't see or hear him anymore."

A flutter of wings stirred the mist, and Boo came into view. He swung his head back and forth as he settled by Theo's feet. "I tried to hang onto him, but he shook me off."

A deep, frenzied laughter rose within the wind, echoing from every direction, and the marsh came alive at Lesnik's command. The moss was violently jostled, tossing Theo and Boo upward and downward and side to side, like rag dolls on a trampoline. At any moment, Theo felt as if he'd be hurled into the water. He dug his fingers into the moss and held on with all his might.

As suddenly as it had begun, the wind subsided, the mist cleared, and the undulating path settled back to its tranquil state. Theo breathed heavily as he tried to coax his racing heart to beat normally.

"Welcome to the party," a throaty voice said.

Theo shook himself off and looked toward the sound. Anger surged through him. Lord Vodnik sat around a tree stump, with Lesnik on the opposite side. Lord Vodnik was dealing cards for himself and his friend. On the mossy ground by their sides lay a dozen or so empty bottles.

Shaking his head, Theo stomped toward the two creatures. "My sister's dying, and you're here drinking, gambling, and playing stupid games with me, instead of giving me the help I need. I would have had better luck asking Baba Yaga for her assistance."

Lord Vodnik held his webbed paw out toward Theo. "Not now. I need to concentrate."

Anger burned Theo's blood. He swiped the cards off of the table, sending them flying into the murky water. Diamonds, hearts, and spades spun in circles.

Theo scoffed. "There's not a single club. You're not even playing with a full deck. And I'm not just talking about the cards."

Lord Vodnik shivered. "Never, never clubs. They burn to the touch."

"Only my trusty club." Lesnik hiccuped and held aloft a wooden cudgel.

Boo hopped around. "He's not dry now. No need for beer."

Lesnik opened his eyes wide, slurring his words. "You gots it from 'er?"

"No, I didn't 'gots' it from your wife." Theo shook his head in disgust. "And I'm not going to. What you should really do is go home and let her know you're alive. She misses you."

Boo bobbed his beak up and down, agreeing with Theo.

"Don't either of you care at all what happens to Zmeykovo? What happens to Diva?" Theo pointed a finger at Lesnik. "You of all people should care. Lamia destroys everything. You tend to the forests and animals. Doesn't it bother you that she's burning them and killing everything that lives here? You should be ashamed of yourself for how you're behaving."

Lesnik shrugged, but lowered his head.

"Bravo!" Lord Vodnik clapped. "Glad to see you've got some spunk. Lesnik was needing a good scolding. He cheats terribly at cards. Perhaps I'll assist you after all. But it would be nice if you had something to offer me in return."

"Here." Theo thrust the Samodiva belt buckle toward the water lord.

He turned it all around with his webbed paws and licked at the rubies. His eyes glowed.

"A fine piece of workmanship. This will do." He clutched the reward. "So, you're wanting to know where Magda is hiding, eh? That's what Lesnik told me."

"Yes." Theo paced the path. "She has things I need back, so we can save Diva. My mother thought—"

"Yes, yes. No need to go into that." Lord Vodnik waved his hand, dismissing Theo. "Zunitza wasn't thinking straight. We all know what Magda was always after."

Lesnik snickered. "Everything your mother had."

Theo gave the creature a sour look, but clamped his mouth shut. He'd said enough. Now, he wanted answers.

"True, true." Lord Vodnik stroked his green whiskers. "Magda wouldn't go somewhere she and your mother had *good* times …"

"You think Magda went someplace the two of them had *bad* times?" Theo asked.

"No, no. Think harder."

Theo shouted, "I don't want to think. I want to know where Magda is hiding!"

"I told you he had a temper," Lesnik whispered overly loud.

Theo gritted his teeth.

"My boy, you'll feel much better about yourself if you can figure it out," Lord Vodnik added.

"No. I. Won't," Theo screamed. "I just want to know so I can save my sister!"

Boo ruffled his feathers. "Tell him. Tell him. No more games."

"You two are no fun." Lord Vodnik's huge green belly rumbled with laughter. "Oh, fine. She'll be somewhere that was special to your mother and *father*, not somewhere your mother thought fondly of her sister."

"Of course." Theo wacked his head. Magda wanted to be Zunitza. "And do you know where that is?"

Lesnik laughed. "If we knew that, it wouldn't be a special, secret place."

Theo threw his hands up into the air. "I've had enough of you two. If you could tell me the quickest way to get out of this madhouse, I'll let you get back to your game."

Lord Vodnik pointed to a gap between two mossy-covered trees. "You're at the same place where you first stepped into my kingdom."

Theo peered through the trees, and it was true. The river that marked their earlier entrance flowed beyond the marsh. Lesnik had taken them on another merry chase, only to bring Theo back to where he could have gotten answers right away.

"Thanks for wasting my time." He strode down the path and shouted back to the two buddies, "Just for that, I'm going to make sure Kikimora knows exactly where you've been, Lesnik, and what you've been doing."

"No! Don't do it," the forest protector shouted. "You mustn't tell her you've seen me."

Despite his threat, Theo had no plan to saddle Kikimora with the antics of her despicable husband. She deserved better than that. He could visit her himself, to help lessen her loneliness, even if Pavel never wanted to venture into that part of the marsh again.

When Theo stepped out of the marsh, he inhaled a deep breath of fresh air to clear his mind.

Boo rubbed his head against Theo's ankle. "What will you do now?"

"Let me see if I can contact my mother." Theo closed his eyes and spoke in his mind, *"Mom, can you hear me? Magda wasn't in your hiding places. Can you tell me somewhere that was special to you and Dad? Some place Magda might know of, but other people don't?"*

Zunitza's voice came back barely a whisper. *"Where your father and I first met. He can show you."*

With that, she was gone. Theo had to approach his father and interrupt his plans for war. But if Theo was correct in his thinking, they would find the Golden Apple with Magda and avert war.

Surely, she hasn't given it to Lamia?

Theo was positive that at least Magda wouldn't have taken Zunitza's robe and belt to Kaleto Fortress. His aunt had to have more sense than trust Lamia with those.

"Theo?" Boo poked Theo's leg with his beak. "What did she say?"

Theo told his feathered friend. "Thank you for coming with me. I can reach my father safely. Will you go back and tell Ula and Pavel everything that's happened?"

"I will. I will." Boo hopped around. "I'm a good messenger."

"And, Boo." Theo hesitated, his words sticking in his throat. "Please look for me if … Diva doesn't make it."

Boo nudged Theo's leg with his beak. "Yes, but I have faith in you. You will succeed."

"I hope you're right."

The magpie pecked at a few bugs on the ground, and then he flew off in the direction of Samodivi Fortress.

Theo shifted into a dragon and headed for home. It startled him for a moment that "home" was the word that came to mind when he thought about Zmey's castle. He hadn't been in Zmeykovo that long, but the place had become comfortable for him, despite its dangers. He still longed to see his mother and Nia in Selo, but that place was slowly becoming a memory. He feared that returning to the seaside village would revert him to being the unassuming boy he had been while living there. A boy who always walked in other people's shadows.

Zmeykovo was where he belonged now. With a family he had once thought was only mythical. He had so many plans to help the inhabitants. But he needed Diva by his side.

He hoped he could convince his father to set aside his war plans momentarily and go to the secret rendezvous place that was so special to him and Zunitza. If not, Theo would go it alone. He wouldn't stop until Diva was well—no matter the cost.

Chapter 5
Mysterious Wizards

AN UNUSUAL FLURRY of activity greeted Theo as he passed through the castle corridors. Household staff members were removing statues and artwork from rooms, carrying the items covered with white cloths. Others were taking down hallway decorations and dusting now-unoccupied areas.

Theo stopped a woman lugging a potted plant. "What's going on?"

She set the plant onto the floor and wiped her brow. "Zmey told us to prepare for war, even as he is making plans to attack Kaleto Fortress."

"I'm sure he meant for you to hide, not to save plants and paintings," Theo said. "Things can be replaced. People can't."

"It was not commanded, my prince. It is something we choose to do for him," the woman said. "We are safe here as long as Zmey is in the castle. He expects his sister will send her troops here to finish him off …" She cast her eyes down. "And you, too."

"I can take care of myself." He tapped the sword at his side. "And so can Zmey."

"A sword may not help, my prince. Zmey believes his enemies will try to trap him the way they did before."

Theo remembered what his father had said about how Lamia and Zlo had captured him. They burned a field of komuniga, a plant that was illegal to have in Zmeykovo, because a high dose was toxic to dragons. Zmey was wise to their plans now, however, and they wouldn't trick him that way again.

"Do you know where my father is? I have something urgent to talk with him about."

"He's in the Chamber Room, my prince."

"Thank you." Theo felt bad leaving her with the heavy plant, but his task at hand was pressing.

He couldn't help wondering why his father was in the Chamber Room. That was where Zmey and the Colobari had hidden the Golden Apple. From what Theo remembered, the room wouldn't hold all the Samodivi and Kukeri. Why weren't they in the more spacious study instead? That room afforded them plenty of places to sit or even stand to discuss their battle strategy.

The farther Theo traveled into the heart of the castle, the quieter it became. His footsteps echoed down the corridors as he raced to reach his father. Each footfall seemed to say, "Hurry, hurry." When he reached his destination, Theo placed his hand on the door, but didn't open it. No sounds came from inside.

Are my father and the others really in there? Or have they already moved somewhere else?

He turned the knob. The door was unlocked. His father had to be in the room. He was the only one with a key. Theo inched the heavy door open. The aroma of old books and incense drifted out. It reminded him of the scents in the church in Selo. Theo closed the door behind him and leaned against the entrance.

The windowless room was semi-dark, with shadows lurking where they could. Flickering light from torches mounted in sconces cast a soft glow, catching the lazy dance of dust particles as they drifted past, disturbed by Theo's entrance.

Only Zmey occupied the room. He projected the confidence of king now, not the mournful father who'd moments before had lost his child to treachery. Zmey was adorned in a resplendent white jacket embroidered in gold with intricate symbols. Theo had seen similar images in the book Jabalaka had lent him. They were the sign of nobility.

The dragon king stood deathly still in front of a dark-wooded, star-shaped table set in the center of the room. Equidistant around the table from Zmey were three bird statues: a golden eagle, a silver falcon, and a bronze hawk.

Theo's father raised his hands high above his head. Soft sounds came from his lips, but Theo couldn't make out the words. Despite his eagerness to talk with his father, Theo didn't want to interrupt what appeared to be a solemn ceremony. Instead, he looked around the room whose secrets and mysteries he'd been so eager to uncover. When he and Zmey had come here before, looking for the Golden Apple, Theo had been too upset to take time to thoroughly examine the area.

Seven columns encircled the room, supporting the domed ceiling. He trailed his fingers over the smooth, intricate relief on the nearest column. It held an air of mystique and grandeur. The designs not only displayed patterns he'd come across in the ancient books he'd been reading, but also depicted the beings of Zmeykovo. The column he touched held symbols Diva had tattooed on her arms, as well as scenes of the Samodivi as they hunted, danced, and performed various rituals.

The next column represented the Rusalki and their water kingdom. Another one embodied dragons in all their might and glory. On the column directly across from Theo, the Znahar Tree blazed with golden colors. Surrounding the tree, white-robed people venerated the Thracian deities of Bendis and Tangra. The remaining columns portrayed the Kukeri, the Vodnik community, and the Ispolini, the giants of long ago.

On the domed ceiling, colorful frescoes merged into one another, depicting dragons, celestial bodies, and more ancient symbols. Theo dropped his gaze to room level. Bookcases made of reddish wood lined the walls. The shelves overflowed with old, worn tomes and yellowing scrolls. Some books were bound in leather, while faded cloth covered others. Theo breathed in their scent. Diva would love this room. It was filled with a mysterious aura of knowledge and history.

Zmey's chanting became louder, and Theo turned his attention back to his father. Something was about to happen.

The dragon king's words became distinct. "O Tangra, God of Light, hear my plea and witness this sacred ritual. I again call forth your servants to aid us in our hour of need."

Silence settled over the chamber, and sparks flickered around the statues. Theo held his breath in anticipation as an ethereal presence permeated the room, dispelling shadows.

The dragon king uncorked a vial and poured a sweet-smelling elixir over the statues. As the liquid cascaded down their delicate etchings, it bathed them in a glowing light. The cold metals appeared to expand and contract, as if the breath of life was being infused into them. A surge of power filled the room.

Once more, Zmey raised his arms and waved his hands in a circular motion as he beseeched Tangra's aid. A whirlwind of white light exploded from the statues and engulfed the room. The gold, silver, and bronze shimmered and wavered, melting before Theo's eyes as if heated by a blazing fire. The light that raced throughout the room roared. Theo tore his eyes away from the statues as the light funneled into a beam and lit the dome. Theo blinked back the stars that clouded his vision.

When he regained his sight, he blinked again, not sure what he was seeing was real. Three tall, slender men clothed in hooded white robes stood where the bird statues had been. The men stretched and blinked, freed from their metal confines.

Each man carried an intricately designed staff, one made of gold, another of silver, and the third of bronze—just like the statues had been. The top of each staff formed the Celestial Turtle with its limbs outstretched as if swimming or perhaps even holding up the weight of the world.

Are these the three men who visited my father earlier and convinced him to give me a decoy Golden Apple? The Colobari?

Theo recalled following one of the men to Zmey's treasure room. The man had disappeared, but he had left Theo a message on a piece of parchment: *Follow your fate, Young Dragon Prince, and you will succeed.*

The men removed their hoods as one. Their faces were ageless, showing signs of youth and maturity all at once, but Theo suspected the men were ancient. They had a blend of human and avian features. Theo couldn't help but be drawn first to the men's deep-amber to golden-yellow eyes with large pupils. Their orbs held the piercing, calculating look of birds of prey, but also possessed a hint of curiosity as they returned Theo's gaze. Their noses were slender and delicately curved. The man at the end, farthest from Zmey, who had been a hawk statue only moments before had a subtle flare to his nostrils as if in recognition of Theo. That Colobar, for Theo was certain now that's who the men were, curled up the corners of his thin, tapered lips in what Theo hoped was a friendly smile.

Was he the one I followed to Zmey's treasure trove?

While Zmey conversed with the men in a low voice, Theo continued his observation of the man. The hawk-man had a low forehead, pronounced cheekbones, and tapered jawline. In all, his appearance was graceful and elegant.

The man leaned forward, speaking soft words to Zmey, who turned slowly to acknowledge his son. "Theo, I'm sorry to keep you waiting. How is Diva doing?"

"She's the same, but we made her comfortable in her room in Samodivi Fortress."

"Thank you, son, for being with her." Zmey waved Theo closer. "I'd like to present you officially to the Colobari, my advisers, the great wizards of the White Light." He gestured to the men individually. "Kobur, Tagan, and Rattan. I've summoned them to assist us in the war against Zlo and Lamia."

The men nodded, acknowledging Theo's presence.

Theo took a breath to say more, but Zmey turned back to the statues-turned-men. "When we retrieve the Golden Apple from my sister, we must use it to save my daughter. I'll need you to perform the restoration ritual on it."

"We are at your service, our king," the men said in unison. They raised their staffs and touched the tips over their hearts. "Our power, wisdom, and lives are yours to command."

"Father, about Diva …"

"Yes?" Zmey raised his eyebrows.

"I know you said you didn't think Mom's robe and belt would cure Diva, but …" Theo took a deep breath. "I think I know where Magda took them."

Zmey's face went tense. "We can deal with Magda after we get the Golden Apple."

"I don't think … and Ula doesn't think Diva will last that long." Theo fidgeted with his hands. He'd been chasing too many demons already today. He had to convince his father that this was the top priority. "I think the robe and belt are our best chance of saving my sister."

"Theo …" Zmey paced the room. "I can't go chasing after ideas that *might* work. I *know* the Golden Apple will. With the help of the Colobari. We can't be wasting time trying to find Magda."

Theo wasn't going to give up. He also *knew* in his heart that Zunitza's attire would cure Diva in time. "You can't, but I can."

"Very well." Zmey sighed. "I'll trust your judgment. If you believe with your heart, go look for Magda."

"Thank you." Theo lowered his head to the man who stood before him as king, and not a father. "I need to know where you first met Mom. That's where I believe Magda is hiding."

Zmey paled, and his eyes grew hard and glazed-over. "She can't be there. How dare she defile that place that meant so much to your mother and me?"

"Because she wants *to be* Mom."

The turmoil in Zmey's face broke Theo's heart. He could tell his father was reliving memories. Likely tortured memories of things Magda—and probably Lamia—had done to hurt his beloved Zunitza. Zmey's pale face turned red with anger.

"She won't get away with this," he said, as if talking to himself and not to his son. "I'll never have her. She never was and never could be Zunitza."

"Father." Theo touched Zmey's forearm. "This is urgent. Please tell me how to find your secret place."

Zmey focused on Theo. "Yes. Yes, of course. I can give you a map." He glanced at the Colobari. "We, too, have urgent matters. We must gather these scrolls and bring them to the others. The Samodivi and Kukeri will be waiting for us in the subterranean library."

"Library?" Theo felt the blood drain from his face. Jabalaka was in that library. "Oh, no!"

He rushed out of the room, sped through the castle, and made a mad dash to the rose garden. The only way he might beat the others to the library and warn Jabalaka was to travel down the passageway hidden beneath the gazebo, the entrance Sly used when he went to help his "Master," as the Vodnik called Jabalaka.

Chapter 6
Discovery

A PIERCING SCREAM reached Theo's ears as he scrambled down the tunnel from the gazebo to the underground library. He couldn't tell if it came from Jabalaka or Sly. Whatever the source, Theo had failed to warn his old friend in time about the people coming to the library.

Will Jabalaka escape and find another place to hide before I get a chance to tell him I didn't betray his location?

Out of breath, Theo ran into the room.

Screams, shouts, and utter chaos met him.

Piles of books lay toppled, strewn across the floor. Papers spiraled through the air and drifted down to settle around tables and chairs. The Samodivi had their arrows nocked, pointing to all areas of the massive room, as if preparing for an attack from any direction. And the Kukeri gripped their spears. The bells on their waists clanged loudly as the men danced around the room, looking for the hidden enemy.

Sly hopped from one spot to the next, slipping under tables and darting among the Kukeri and Samodivi, all the while shouting, "Master, Master, hide. Enemy here to kill you. Sly not tell anyone."

Theo felt the Vodnik's panic and apprehension at being accused of giving away Jabalaka's hiding place. The former Keeper of Secrets was nowhere to be seen. Had he already abandoned the library? He must have had another secret exit he hadn't told Theo about.

While everyone else stood stunned and apprehensive, Theo snuck into the smaller library room and closed the door behind him. Maybe his friend was still around.

"Jabalaka? It's Theo." He paused, waiting for the man to reply. "I don't know what started all that commotion, but it's only friends and family out there. The Samodivi and Kukeri—"

A head popped out from behind a stack of books. "My sons? Not Lamia's soldiers?"

Theo nodded, heaving a sigh of relief that Jabalaka was okay. "Neither Sly nor I told anyone you were here. My father sent the others down to prepare for war against Lamia and Zlo."

Jabalaka crept out from his hiding place. The Kuker's faced had paled, and he trembled. After all the torment and torture the man had been through, Theo could understand his fear at being discovered.

"I … I can't hide any longer." Jabalaka sighed. "If your father is well, I feel secure. I don't think Lamia will be able to capture me again."

"Are you ready to reunite with your family?"

Jabalaka nodded.

Theo took hold of Jabalaka's arm and led him into the main library room. Sly continued to scream and run around the room, warning his "Master" of the dangers.

"Sly!" Jabalaka shouted above the noise.

Sly stopped mid-rant. The Vodnik ran-hopped toward Jabalaka. "No, Master. Hide!"

An unearthly silence followed, as everyone turned their eyes in Jabalaka's direction. That quiet lasted only a moment, turning into boisterous shouts as everyone recognized Jabalaka.

"You're alive!"

"We thought you were dead!"

"What are you doing here?"

More words Theo couldn't distinguish rang out as voices shouted all around the library.

The Kukeri rushed over and grabbed their father, squeezing him tight.

Jabalaka's face turned from pale to red, and he wheezed because of the suffocating embraces. "Well, I'm going to be dead if all of you don't let me breathe. Is that any way to treat your father?"

One by one, the Kukeri released their hold on Jabalaka and stepped away. Their faces told their varied emotions: surprise, joy, anger, relief, and so much more.

Jega remained by his father's side and said the words Theo was sure all of Jabalaka's sons were feeling. "You trusted the Vodnik and Theo with your secret, but not your own sons?"

Theo started to protest his innocence, but Jabalaka held his hand out to stop the words. "My dear friend Sly found my hiding place quite by accident." Jabalaka motioned for the Vodnik to come to his side. "But he has proven himself useful and a trusted ally."

"So, I suppose Sly then told Theo where you were," another of the brothers said. "We all know how the Vodnik venerates the young prince."

Sly's bulbous eyes darted back and forth between Theo and the Kuker. "Sly no tell anyone. Sly keeps secrets."

"No, Sly didn't tell me," Theo said. "I found the library by accident, as well."

"And you couldn't even tell me?" The hurt on Jega's face made Theo cringe. "I thought I was your friend, too."

"You are." Theo stepped toward Jega. "I know you're hurting now because of Zi …" Theo couldn't say the word when Jega flinched. "Because you lost your brother. You all are." Theo looked at each of the Kukeri brothers in turn. "But don't you think Jabalaka's safety was more important than letting anyone else know he was alive? And where he was? Lamia has so many spies. If she even *thought* Jabalaka was still alive … Well, could you live with yourselves if she discovered him and tortured or actually killed him this time?"

Jega hung his head. "No. His safety is most important."

"And so it is."

All heads turned to look at Zmey and the Colobari, who had entered the library.

"We'll make sure our illustrious Keeper of Secrets remains safe." Zmey strode toward Jabalaka and clasped the man on both shoulders. "Welcome back to the land of the living, my friend. The Colobari only just now told me how you've been hiding here."

Theo opened his eyes wide. "They knew, too?"

Rattan, the hawk-man, nodded. "We have our ways."

"Then …" Theo snuck a glance at Jabalaka. "Then the Keeper was never safe here? If others knew …"

"He was perfectly safe," Rattan replied. "Safer specifically because we *did* know."

The man's piercing eyes penetrated into Theo. He shivered as he felt tingling in his mind, as if the Colobar was determining Theo's fate, still judging whether he would be a worthy successor to Zmey. Theo believed his father's assessment that the men were trusted priests of the supreme god, Tangra. Yet, still … the men lacked the warmth and compassion of the priestess, Kosara. Perhaps it was their ability to predict favorable times for battle, which distinguished them from Kosara, that made them appear more formidable. Their raptor-like eyes didn't help the Colobari appear friendlier, either. Even so, Theo didn't feel malice coming from the man, who seemed as curious about Theo as Theo was of the man. Perhaps he was probing to discover more about the human world in which Theo had grown up.

The Colobar looked away and joined his brethren, who had laid the scrolls from the Chamber Room out onto a table. The tingling sensation ceased, and Theo breathed a sigh of relief.

Theo approached Zmey. "Father?"

Zmey turned to look at Theo.

Theo tried to keep the anxiety out of his voice, but so much time had been lost. "The map? Please. To your and Mom's secret place."

"Yes, of course." Zmey strode to a shelf, thumbed through scrolls, and pulled out a yellowed one. He unrolled it, nodded to himself, and brought it back. "At the base of Cherna Mountain, go to the foot of the westernmost dragon statue that's perched on the pillars above the waterfall. From there, follow this passageway." Zmey pointed to a location on the map. "It will lead you to the place where I first saw your mother."

"Thank you, Father." Theo took the scroll and turned to leave.

"One more thing," Zmey said. "Seek out Baba Yaga's help. If Magda is truly there, you will need the witch's assistance. Your mother's sister is powerful enough to twist the enchantment of that secret place against you. Baba Yaga can protect you and help you trap Magda."

To his father, Theo said. "I will."

But he groaned inwardly. He'd hoped that his days of depending on Baba Yaga's help had ended. *How much more time am I going to lose now that I have to try to get the witch to help? And what price will she demand this time?*

For Diva's sake, he'd do whatever the witch demanded.

Chapter 7
Secret Rendezvous

THE FOREST OF WHISPERING BELLS announced Theo's arrival long before he set foot in Baba Yaga's glen. As he stood there, the bells continued their chiming. He held his hand just out of reach of the gate latch. Its sharp teeth rattled every time he moved closer. Even the skulls that topped the bone fence blinked fiery eyes as if daring him to continue in his quest.

"Well, you just gonna stand there all day?"

Theo jumped back, drawing his hand to his side.

Baba Yaga walked down the jittery steps from her hut on chicken legs. "Stand still, will ya!" she shouted at the hut. Then she cursed the forest. "Quiet! Can't an old lady have any peace around here?"

"You're no lady," Theo mumbled under his breath.

"What's that?" Baba Yaga hobbled over, poking her nose toward Theo across the still-closed gate. She sniffed, trying to get closer to him, but he backed away.

"So, no uroki this time, I see … or rather smell." She cackled. "If an evil spirit doesn't possess you, what brings you back here already? I've had about enough of you and your wants."

"I … um … I've come at my father's request."

This was the first time—and only time, he hoped—that he'd been to visit Baba Yaga by himself. No Diva to help soothe the cranky witch's moods. No Pavel to make her laugh. Just Theo. And he and the witch had bad karma. Not least of all because of the tricks she played. Theo thought about how he'd left Baba Yaga stranded in the Kaleto Fortress torture room. How he'd had the witch gagged and blindfolded so she wouldn't know the way to the treasure room. How he continued to speak roughly to her.

Had any of that been necessary? He nodded to himself. Yes. She was a trickster and couldn't be trusted. Yet … she had been with his father when he needed her, and Zmey continued to speak highly of the witch, so she must have good qualities. Theo had yet to see much of them, however.

"Well?" Baba Yaga rattled the gate. "What is your father's request? Don't keep me waiting all day."

Theo found himself opening up to the witch. He poured out the story of what had happened since their failed attempt to resurrect Diva. He talked about all the wasted time with Lesnik, which got him a "He he, ho ho, so that's where he's been hiding" from Baba Yaga. He talked about the Colobari, Magda, and the secret meeting place.

Having released all of his pent-up frustration, he took a deep breath. "So, will you help me trap Magda?"

Baba Yaga tugged at a wiry gray hair sticking out of her chin. "Lemme see, lemme see."

Anger rose in Theo. "Don't tell me you want something in return again."

"No, dragon boy, I don't want anything. I'll gladly do what your father asks." The witch held her head up and straightened her bent-over back as best she could. "I was deciding whether to give you a potion or charm or …" Here she grinned. "Or come with you to watch all the fun."

Theo groaned. It was bad enough having to deal with the witch. Now, he might have to put up with her presence when he needed to concentrate on overpowering Magda to retrieve the robe and belt.

"Yes, I think that will be best." Baba Yaga hopped around, a big smirk on her face. "No sense trusting you to do what I tell you when I can do it myself. Well, times a wasting. I must get what I'll need." She scrambled up the hut steps.

Theo slapped his head. "I can do this. I can deal with the witch for however long it takes if it means we can save Diva."

A purple cat flew out of the hut and landed by Theo.

Theo gently pushed her away with his foot. "Ah, Kotka, what do you want? Don't scratch me."

The cat purred and rubbed herself around Theo's ankles. He tensed as she wound in and out, over and again. Every moment, he expected the claws to come out and the cat to begin hissing.

"He he, ho ho." Baba Yaga, with overflowing pouch in hand, made her way down the steps. "My Kotka likes you now. I guess that means I really do have to help." She hopped into the mortar and stirred the wind with her pestle. "Come, Kotka. We're off on an adventure."

The cat gave Theo one more rub before she flew and nestled onto the edge of the mortar.

"There's room for you in here, too." Baba Yaga pointed at Theo.

"Ah, no. I'd rather fly there myself."

She shrugged. "Suit yourself. If you want to eat the fumes of my old Chutura that's your business." Under her breath she mumbled, "Don't know when those Samodivi will give me the new one they promised."

Theo told the witch the location.

"See you there," she cackled as she shot off into the air. Black puffs of smoke trailed her.

Theo closed his eyes. "I can do this. I can do this. It won't be so bad."

He shifted into dragon form and followed Baba Yaga.

Despite his anxiety, he felt a sense of freedom and exhilaration each time he flew. The ability to do the one thing that had long been his desire. To soar through the sky.

I wonder if Diva can shift into a dragon?

He smiled to himself when he thought about the time he'd been caught trying to shift into a bird the way Diva did. Back then, they all had believed that only Samodivi could do this. Females, not males. If he was the exception to the rule, then it was likely Diva was, too. So, she should be able to shift into a dragon, as well.

How different will it be for her to become a dragon, instead of a bird? Will she be able to fly gracefully that way? Or will the difference in weight make it difficult?

He had to believe that Diva would have the chance to try. Magda would be stopped. Lamia would be stopped. Zlo would be stopped. Then everything in Zmeykovo could return to normal.

Theo's heart raced as he neared the dragon statue. The only other time he'd seen it had been from the ground on the other side of the lake. Now, flying as a dragon himself, he circled the statue up close, while he looked for a place to land at the base of the waterfall where Baba Yaga waited.

What he'd originally thought were two statues of dragons ready to battle each other now appeared to be creatures spreading their wings to protect a pair of eggs. The dragons' tails wrapped protectively around the eggs and wound their way down the pillar. Each dragon looked lovingly at the egg it guarded.

Because he had more pressing matters to deal with, Theo tore his eyes away from the statues and circled down toward Baba Yaga. She was drumming her fingers against the side of her mortar.

"Took ya long enough," she shouted above the roar of the waterfall. "Thought you were in a hurry."

"I am," he said after he shifted into boy form. "Let's go."

He retrieved the map his father had given him and ducked into a narrow tunnel. Baba Yaga started her mortar and followed behind, but Kotka flew ahead of both of them. The farther they traveled, the darker the passageway became. Theo's dragon vision enabled him to read the map and avoid debris along the way. Baba Yaga didn't fare as well. Grunts and curses came from her as the witch bumped and scraped against the ground and walls.

At each junction, Kotka flew in circles. She hissed at Theo as if she, too, was telling him to hurry up so she knew which way to go. They continued on, turning down one passageway after another, until a ray of light shown ahead. Kotka zipped past Theo and disappeared into what must be their destination.

A moment later, the cat yowled and shot back down the tunnel. Howling and with her claws extended, she circled Theo and Baba Yaga.

"What's gotten into you, silly beast?" the witch shouted and swatted the cat.

Ungodly noises spewed out of Kotka's mouth.

"Whatever it was, we're not going to surprise it now with all that noise." Theo hurried toward the light.

Clutching his sword, he stepped out of the tunnel. Rushing water and the soothing sounds of nature greeted him. He kept his back against the stone wall as he surveyed the area, looking for whatever monster had startled Kotka.

On the rocky cliff at the opposite side of the glen, a waterfall cascaded into a lake. The water sparkled with rosy hues as it reflected the remnants of daylight. Spray from the waterfall created a mist that spread out across the terrain, making the air cool and refreshing. Fine-tuning his dragon vision, Theo honed in on the area behind the waterfall, searching for anything malicious lurking there.

Nothing.

His search continued along the pristine sandy beach. No feet had disturbed a path along it any time recently. Next, he concentrated on the lush greenery nestled around the lake. Still nothing evil made his dragon senses tingle.

He'd set foot into a peaceful sanctuary within the confines of the mountains.

Theo turned to look back down the tunnel, where Baba Yaga held a trembling Kotka.

"You can come out," Theo said. "This is just another wasted trip. No one is here. I don't know what scared your cat."

"Don't be so hasty." Baba Yaga flew into the open space. She set Kotka on the ground and hobbled out of her mortar. She sniffed the air. "Some things will remain hidden to you that a witch as powerful as I am can sniff out."

"So, you're telling me Magda is here?" Theo sent out his dragon senses again, but couldn't detect any malicious vibes.

"Something's here." Baba Yaga lugged her pouch toward a circle of rocks and set it down. "This will do."

She pulled out jars and white candles, muttering as she did. "Black pig grease. Hemp. Poppy seeds. Rue. Belladonna. Basil. Rosemary." On and on she rambled. "Ah, there it is. Toad skin," she said as she pulled out a final item.

Theo held his hand in front of his mouth, ready to gag. "You could have had your supper before you left."

"It's not to eat." The witch put her hands on her hips. "You want my help or not?"

He lowered his head. "Yes, sorry. What do you need all that stuff for?"

"An ointment to put me into a trance. It'll help me see what's hiding here." She arranged the candles in a circle by the rocks. "I have to rub it onto my naked body—"

"What?" Theo backed away. "No way."

Baba Yaga cackled. "The alternative is I'll rub it on my forehead, and you'll have to keep your hand there, so I can transmit to you what I see."

Theo shivered at the thought of touching her, but that was better than … No, he didn't want that image imprinted on his brain.

"You should be honored," Baba Yaga said. "This ointment is used only rarely. It has to be a special occasion."

"How did you know this"—he spread his hands wide, pointing at the assortment of jars—"was what you needed?"

"Your aunt cloaks all her deeds and intents." Baba Yaga placed the candles around the inside of the circle of rocks and lit them. "If Magda came here, to a place that meant something to your mother and father, then she came here to relive a moment that was special to Zmey and Zunitza. But Magda can live out that event only in a trance. So, to catch her, we'll have to enter that same state of mind."

"Oh." Theo didn't know what else to say. "What do you need me to do?"

"Come sit here, inside the circle, next to me."

The witch patted the ground while she added the ingredients into a household-sized mortar and ground the herbs into the grease with a pestle. She dug her crooked fingers into the mixture, bringing out globs, which she smeared onto her forehead. Next, she closed her eyes, and took a few deep breaths.

"Place your hand over the ointment," she said.

He gritted his teeth but did as she requested. *I'm doing this for Diva*, he kept repeating to himself.

"Now," Baba Yaga continued, "imagine that a sphere of white protective light surrounds you. It'll shield you from any counter-attack Magda may hurl at you when she discovers you've entered her realm."

Theo closed his eyes. A white glow appeared at the back of his eyes and grew. It spread across his face, down his shoulders, extending out to his arms. Next, it covered his torso and crept over his legs. Around the edges, a rainbow of colors formed.

"*Mom?*" he thought, feeling her gentle touch.

Zunitza had added her own protection around him.

Baba Yaga began to chant an incantation. "By the ancient Thracian spirits, I seek to see. A hidden event unfold before me. Grant me visions deep and clear. Protection from all harm I hold dear."

Theo began to feel lightheaded. His vision blurred, and he surrendered himself to the experience. Mist shrouded him and Baba Yaga. Their spirits left their bodies, and Baba Yaga tore the mist aside like opening curtains to let in the morning sunshine.

Theo blinked. A shadowy figure formed across the lake. A woman sat on a smooth, moss-covered boulder. The mist from the waterfall surrounded her. She wore a long, white, flowing robe that shimmered in the remaining sunlight that filtered through the trees. A golden belt encircled her waist. The woman rose, slid off of the rock, and danced.

Someone next to Theo sighed.

He spun around. A vision of his father had entered the glen. Theo could sense Zmey's thoughts. It was love at first sight. He took a step toward the woman but stopped when she began to sing a haunting, beautiful tune, that blended into perfect harmony with the gentle hum of the waterfall. Her voice was as sweet and lovely as her surroundings. The words of the song spoke of joy and wonder and celebrated the beauty of the forest and the creatures that lived within it.

A smile crossed the vision-Zmey's face. His thoughts were clear to Theo. The song connected the dragon king to an even deeper level to the woman whose name he did not yet know. The connection went beyond words. It was as if she were a part of him, the missing half his soul longed to reunite with.

As he listened with his heart and soul, a six-winged deer with a shimmering motley coat pranced out of the tree line toward the woman. White spots like stars freckled his back. Theo immediately recognized Shar, who'd once been his mother's deer and now was Theo's companion. Here, Shar appeared more carefree, flapping his wings in what appeared to be a playful mood.

The creature Theo had come to know was more serious. A bit of that showed through the vision-creature's deep-set eyes, filled with wisdom. Those eyes now radiated a sense of calm and serenity as his globe sparkled with soft green light. Theo had never witnessed that color on the Shar he knew. That deer had suffered a great loss when Zunitza died.

The vision-Zmey thought, *I could stay here for hours.* And he did, lost in the woman's world of wonder and beauty. Zmey remained rooted to his hidden location, not daring to speak to the enchanting nymph who had stolen his heart. To move, to speak would spoil the tranquility of the forest and the magic of the waterfall. He wanted to savor the moment.

Zmey left only when the sun set and stars decorated the heavens. In his heart, he knew he'd meet his soulmate again and they'd be together forever. They would always have one another, even if death came for one before the other.

Although it was hours in the vision, the sun remained steadfast in the world where Theo's body rested next to Baba Yaga. He blinked away tears. Both Zmey's and Zunitza's sisters had other plans for the loving couple. Theo's aunts had brought so much pain to Zmeykovo. He wasn't going to let it continue through to his generation.

The vision became blurry. A woman still danced, but now she wore a wedding gown covered with golden coins. The same one Theo had seen in the cupboard in his father's room. Zunitza's wedding gown.

Theo's heart raced. Was the woman a vision of his mother? A memory imprinted in this space she held so dear? Or had Magda imagined herself to be Zunitza?

The rainbow glow tightened around Theo, assuring him that the woman he saw was no longer his mother.

He screamed, "Magda!"

Baba Yaga went limp, her breathing heavy.

Theo tore his hand from the witch's forehead. He jumped up and raced toward his deceitful aunt. Before he reached her, a shadow eclipsed what remained of the sunshine, and a piercing screech came from above.

Chapter 8
A Mother's Love

A MASSIVE WHITE VULTURE circled overhead. Its wingspan was at least three times wider than the tunnel's entrance. With another screech, the monster lunged toward Theo. He pulled out his sword from the scabbard.

The vulture must be what terrified Kotka earlier.

This beast was likely the one Theo had encountered once before. A giant vulture had seized a living bull in front of his eyes and carried it off. Whether the vulture wanted the animal for food or not was debatable. Theo thought Lamia had commanded the scavenger to thwart his and his friends' mission to fight the ferocious Water Bull. Defeating that monster had enabled them to find the passageway that eventually led them to where Zmey had been imprisoned.

Now, the vulture was back.

What does it want? Is it now obeying Magda's commands and protecting her?

Theo thrust his sword at the vulture as it approached with its talons extended, aiming for Theo's face. The creature dodged the weapon and swooped past. Again, it dove toward Theo, reaching its talons toward his neck. One claw snagged the chain that held Theo's seven-pointed star medallion. The chain broke, and the medallion soared through the air to land by the water's edge.

"Oh, no, you don't." Theo dashed toward the lake. *What terrible thing do they want to use my medallion for now?*

Zlo had needed it in the ritual that brought Lamia back to life and opened a portal for his demons. Theo wasn't going to let anything like that happen again. He grabbed the medallion, and in one swift motion shifted into dragon form. Now, the medallion was tattooed upon his chest, safe from the vulture's clutches.

The beast remained relentless in its attacks nonetheless, as if something else motivated it to fight.

Revenge? Was the vulture trying to make Theo pay for killing its mate on his first trip to Zmeykovo? Theo hadn't wanted to kill that vulture, but it had attacked Diva. He had to protect her. His aim with the bow and arrow had been so terrible when he practiced, he hadn't been certain that the arrow would fly true and kill the giant beast.

Now, once more, he had to battle the monster so he could save Diva's life. Time was running out. He had to act quickly to not only chase off the beast but also fight Magda to get back his mother's robe and belt.

Magda! His thoughts returned to her. *Has she already made her escape?*

He turned to where his aunt had been before the vulture attacked. In that brief moment, the creature found the perfect opportunity to strike. Its claws tore into Theo's shoulder. He whipped around so fast, the vulture lost its grip and tumbled in the sky.

Throbbing pain raced through Theo's body, and he let out a roar. Flames erupted toward the vulture. The beast had already gained control of its movement and soared above the fire. The creature's wings stirred the flames as it circled above. When the flames died, the vulture once more made a beeline for Theo with its talons extended.

Theo pumped his wings and flew backward, narrowly avoiding the attack. He circled around, keeping pace with the vulture, just out of reach. The monster remained relentless. Back and forth it darted, looking for purchase on Theo's scales. Each time Theo shot flames toward the vulture, it veered out of the way of the tongues of fire by diving under Theo.

For some time, they battled in the sky. Attacking. Retreating. A game of hide and seek. Their wings created a whirlwind of ash and feathers.

Enough of this. Theo breathed fire toward the vulture, and then lunged in the opposite direction, where he expected the beast to fly. His guess was correct. Theo slammed his wings into the vulture.

It tottered in the sky. Taking advantage of its disorientation, Theo breathed another long breath toward the vulture. This one struck.

The vulture let out a savage cry. Singed flesh and burning feathers soiled the air. The beast shook its long neck, then turned tail.

Theo had won. The beast retreated.

Now to deal with Magda.

But when he looked where she had been, only empty boulders met his gaze. He searched the glen, but his aunt had disappeared.

He'd failed. Time had run out. He didn't know how he was going to get Zunitza's robe and belt now.

Please don't let Diva die, he begged the Thracian deities.

Frustrated, he landed where he had left Baba Yaga and shifted back to boy form. The witch had recovered from her trance and sat in her mortar, with Kotka in her usual place on the edge.

"That was some show." The witch cackled. "I thought you were a goner a couple of times."

Theo shook his head. "Were you hoping I was? Did you and the cat place bets on the outcome?"

"Nah." Baba Yaga stroked Kotka's fur. "We wouldn't have bet against each other."

Theo didn't know if that meant they would have bet on or against him winning, but he didn't care. He had to find another way—quickly—to help Diva.

"Magda's gone." He sighed. "And the robe and belt with her. Now, how—?"

"Hold on a sec." She leaned into her mortar. "Will these do?"

She pulled out a Samodiva belt, a white robe, and a wedding dress covered with gold coins.

Theo took a step back. "What? How …?" He glanced to where Magda had been dancing earlier, dressed in those very items. "How did you get them?"

"Pfft." She shook her head. "A witch has to keep some tricks to herself. You already know one of my special rituals. Can't let you in on all my secrets."

Theo stepped over to the mortar and ran his fingers along the finely crafted items. "I could hu—"

He shivered. No, he couldn't hug her. It had repulsed him enough to put his hand on her greasy forehead. "We have to get to Samodivi Fortress right now."

Baba Yaga held the garments close to her. "As long as I receive the credit for getting these things back. I might need another favor from the Samodivi one day."

Theo snorted. Same old witch. Always wanting to be one up on everyone. "I don't care about favors. I want to save my SISTER! And we don't have much time left."

The sun had neared the horizon, casting the sky with a red hue. Theo hoped they weren't already too late. He shifted into a dragon and flew above the glen. No need to retreat through the tunnels. Once he was airborne, he could find his way back to the fortress. He didn't worry that the witch would follow him and bring Zunitza's garments. Baba Yaga had the incentive of her potential favors to keep her on track. And he thought she did care a little about Diva.

Once he'd attained enough height, Theo pumped his wings faster than he ever had before. Golden lights from the temple to the south were a blur as adrenaline pushed him onward. Forests sped by in a green haze. He kept his eyes focused on the fortress towers, his heart racing as they grew ever closer.

He kept repeating in his mind, *Please don't be too late. Please don't be too late.*

The ground shook when he landed in the courtyard. He quickly shifted back into a boy and made a mad dash toward the fortress.

No, I have to wait for Baba Yaga to bring the robe and belt. He chastised himself for not taking them with him. Why hadn't he thought of that before? *I can't go in there without them. Ula and Pavel will think I failed, and ... I'm too anxious to tell them everything that happened.*

Theo looked at the sky the way he'd come. Black puffs of smoke from the witch's mortar seemed so far away.

What if I'm already too late? He took another step toward the fortress. *I have to see Diva.*

Again, he pulled back. *No, I need to bring them hope, not despair.* "Come on, witch," he shouted. "Can't you get here faster?"

He paced one end of the courtyard to the other. He had dug grooves in the dirt by the time black puffs of smoke neared the fortress. The moment the mortar touched ground, Theo ran over and stuck his hands inside, pulling out his mother's garments.

"Hey, grabby, be careful," Baba Yaga shrieked as Kotka hissed and flew into the fortress.

Theo was seconds behind the cat. Holding the precious items close to his chest, he sprinted all the way to Diva's room.

Pans of burning incense were spread around the room, emitting an aroma of smil and bay leaves. A golden mist seeped out of a cauldron set over a fire in the hearth. The mist spread around the room, making it moist and humid. Ula must have gone to the lake to get the healing water.

The Samodiva looked up from a chair when Theo stormed into the room. Pavel remained motionless where he sat on the floor holding Diva's hand. His head leaned against the side of the bed. Kotka had already made herself comfortable on Diva's chest. No one had shooed the cat away, but Boo glared at Kotka from the top of a pile of books and shook his head at the cat.

"Is she … Am I too late?" Theo breathed heavily.

"She's still with us, but her essence is so weak." Ula rose and approached Theo. "We thought we'd lost her a couple of times, but Pavel kept talking to her, telling her to hold on."

Theo unclasped his mother's clothing from his tight grip. "I … I got them. The robe and belt."

"Well, actually, I did." Baba Yaga hobbled into the room. "Mighty fine piece of work that was, too."

"Yes, the witch took them from Magda." Theo handed the robe and belt to Ula, but held onto the wedding dress. "Baba Yaga can tell us all about it afterwards if she wants, but right now, we need to perform the ritual."

Pavel looked up, bleary-eyed. A spark of hope glimmered in his eyes. He turned back to Diva. "Hold on a little longer, will ya? Theo's back. You're going to be okay."

Ula removed Kotka and laid the robe over her sister. The cat hissed and skulked to a corner, where she licked her paws.

"What about the belt?" Theo asked. "Magda said it had more power than the robe."

Ula snorted. "Another of her lies. Samodivi belts have power, but the energy coming from our robes is the most potent. You must have heard stories in the human world about men controlling Samodivi when those men have stolen the nymphs' robes."

Theo nodded.

"Your aunt wanted you to mistrust Diva," Ula continued. "Why else would Magda steal Zunitza's belt and blame it on Diva? It was Magda who sought power, not my sister."

Once more, Theo berated himself for falling for Magda's lies. Both his aunts were deceivers. He needed to trust his instincts and not the convincing words Magda and Lamia spewed.

"Let us begin," Ula said. "Everyone, form a circle around Diva and do as I do and repeat what I say."

When they had positioned themselves, Ula lifted her hands and swayed as she began to hum. The golden mist swirled and gathered over Diva. Ula sang words next, not the same as Sava's by the lake. Those words had invoked Bendis, Goddess of the Moon. Instead, Ula poured out her heart directly to Zunitza, to a mother's love.

"Our queen, beloved of all, harken to our call. Behold your daughter lies still, struck down against our will. Lend to her your love, to her spirit that soars above. We beseech your aid. Let not our beloved fade."

Once more she hummed when everyone had repeated her words. Kotka joined in with soft mewls, and Boo made clicking noises with his beak. Ula's slow swaying in place ended, and she began to dance in a circle around Diva's bed. Theo, Pavel, and even Baba Yaga followed after her, although the witch's movements were more hops than graceful steps.

The golden mist swirled around with their movements, and little by little lay completely over Diva. Ula danced faster and sang louder, repeating her words from before. Beside Theo, Baba Yaga wheezed and stumbled. He grabbed one of her hands and Pavel the other. Between them, they kept the witch going, at times, dragging her along. Kotka's mewls turned into yowls, and Boo squawked out sounds Theo had never heard from the magpie. The two animals took to the air, flying in chaotic circles over Diva.

When Theo thought he couldn't hold Baba Yaga any longer, Ula ceased dancing. He dropped the witch's hand, and she bent over, coughing.

Ula raised her hands once more and shouted, "Our queen, beloved of all, harken to our call. Behold your daughter lies still, struck down against our will. Lend to her your love, to her spirit that soars above. We beseech your aid. Let not our beloved fade."

She added one final line to her song. "May the love and light of Zunitza save our beloved, brave Diva!" With that, she tossed silver dust over her sister. It turned into a rainbow of colors when it touched the golden mist. As it settled onto the robe, the garment glowed with a soft white light.

Everyone waited.

Theo held his breath, willing Diva to open her eyes. Across from him, Pavel held his clutched hands in front of his mouth as he mumbled. Ula remained standing where she had stopped. Her lips moved, but no words escaped. Baba Yaga slid to the floor. Her heavy breathing was the only other sound in the room. Kotka flew next to her mistress and lay in the witch's lap, while Boo took one more spin over Diva before flying to land by Theo's feet. The magpie squashed himself up as close as he could.

The glow from the robe dimmed.

Theo counted to a hundred. Waiting for the thumps of Diva's heart to grow louder, more frequent.

But Diva's body didn't move.

"Come on, Diva. Get up," he thought to her, hoping she could hear him again, let him know she was coming back.

He started counting again or else he would scream. The robe had to work. A mother's love was the greatest cure for everything.

The silence in the room was deafening. Even the witch had her breathing under control.

Baba Yaga broke the stillness. "Well, it was worth a try."

"No!" Pavel shouted. "We're not giving up." He hurled himself to Diva's side and grabbed her hand. "Don't leave us!"

The body beneath the robe stirred, and Diva coughed.

Chapter 9
Reunion

THEO BLINKED SEVERAL TIMES. As much as he had wanted it to be true that Diva would revive, he'd been holding back his emotions, expecting disappointment. He'd failed so often in his endeavors in Zmeykovo that he had braced himself in the event he lost Diva permanently. But now, she'd opened her eyes and sat up, a dazed look on her face.

"Diva!" Pavel was the first to engulf her in a hug before she had a chance to say anything.

Boo flew around the room, squawking, "Diva's alive. We did it!"

Kotka sat washing her paws next to her mistress, as if nothing spectacular had just happened. Baba Yaga herself was grinning, and not in her usual creepy way.

"Theo." Ula took his hands in hers.

Bright, unshed tears threatened to spill down her face. Theo could tell they were happy ones because of Ula's big smile.

"Go to her." She nodded toward the bed. "Welcome your sister back."

Theo hesitated, feeling suddenly shy. He couldn't help think about how Diva would react to their newfound relationship. She'd never acted superior to him, even when she thought he was a human. His Samodiva friend—sister, he reminded himself—had always accepted and helped him. But … claiming a blood relationship with another person changed things. He thought about the popular saying that you can choose your friends but not your family. Would Diva be glad they were related? Would she have chosen him to be her brother?

"Theo, go." Ula squeezed his hands before releasing them. "It'll be okay."

He took hesitant steps toward the bed.

"Theo, get this crazy person off of me." Diva struggled to push Pavel away. "What's wrong with you, Pavel? Are you still enchanted by Sirin? I only just woke up. We have to get the Golden Apple back to the castle."

Theo stopped mid-step. *Diva doesn't remember anything! How am I going to explain what happened?*

Pavel let go of Diva. His mouth was slightly open as he looked at her.

She glanced around the room. "How did I get here? All of us? We were at Drakus' cave. And Ula wasn't with us. Am I still dreaming?"

"Dreaming?" Theo asked.

She nodded. "I had this really crazy dream."

Theo sat next to her on the bed. "Maybe you should tell us about it. Then we can answer any questions you have."

"Most of the time, I was walking through the darkness," Diva began. "I heard lots of fighting going on, but I didn't have my bow and arrows with me, so I had to keep looking around to make sure no one attacked me."

"There was—" Pavel started, but Theo shook his head.

"What else?" Theo asked.

"I felt a sharp pain in my chest. After that, I was lying by the water, and everyone was there. You guys. Zmey. My sisters. And lots of others I didn't see but heard."

Theo nodded. "And what else was happening in your … dream?"

"I'm not really sure." She scrunched up her face in thought. "Lots of noise, and the ground was shaking, but then it turned black again. And …" She smiled as she looked at Theo. "You'll think this next part is crazy."

"Maybe not." He smiled back, but his face was tense.

"Okay, you asked for it." She tapped him on the shoulder. "I was wandering through the Forest of Souls. Actually, not wandering. I knew exactly where I wanted to go. To see your mom, my queen, Zunitza."

Theo tightened his grip on the edge of the bed. "What was so crazy about it?"

"You won't believe this. She said …" Diva hesitated. "I know it was just a dream, but she said I'm her daughter and your twin."

Theo felt the blood drain from his face.

Diva laughed. "Don't be scared. It was only a dream. Would it be so bad if we were siblings? Twins? You look like the idea terrifies you."

"No, I—"

"It wasn't a dream," Pavel blurted out. "Theo really is your brother!"

"Ha ha. Funny, Pavel. I'm glad you have your sense of humor again." She turned back to Theo. "It would be amazing if we were twins, don't you think?"

Theo gulped. "I … we … Pavel wasn't …" He didn't know what to say. Would she really think it was cool that they were twins in real life? Or did she say that only because she thought it was a dream?

Baba Yaga chuckled on the floor where she still sat. "Cat got your tongue, dragon boy?"

Ula gave the witch a stern look and sat next to Theo. "Diva," she said, "we have a lot to tell you."

As Ula poured out the story, Theo watched Diva's expressions. She scowled when she learned that Magda had drugged and enchanted her. Theo was sure Diva was wracking her brain wondering how his aunt had been able to do that.

"It was in the water she gave you," Theo said to put Diva's mind at ease.

"A sip? That's all I took." Diva shook her head. "Is Magda that powerful?"

Ula nodded. "I'm afraid so. Only Baba Yaga and the Colobari have more magical powers."

Diva's eyes grew hard as Ula explained how Magda had continued to insist that Diva was a traitor and had gone to Kaleto Fortress and taken the Golden Apple to Lamia—willingly.

"What was her real reason for her wanting *me* to take it?" Diva asked. "She could have just done it herself without all the fuss."

"She needed the blood of an heir to Zmeykovo to complete the ritual and transfer the power of the apple to whomever ate it," Theo said. "They were having no luck getting me there, so they used you."

Diva's eyes grew wide. "That would mean we really are siblings. And they knew it?"

Theo and Ula nodded. On the floor, Baba Yaga cackled.

Ula faced the witch. "There is nothing funny about that."

Theo was glad Ula said it and not him.

"No, no. He he. Can't help myself." Baba Yaga pointed to Diva. "I ain't ever seen her so frazzled. Always so sure of the world. Everything under control. It just struck me as funny."

A disgusted look crossed Ula's face, and she shook her head. Turning back to Diva, she said, "That's where the really terrible part of the story comes in."

Ula proceeded to tell Diva how Magda had drugged Zunitza after she had given birth to Theo. When the second baby came, Zunitza was unaware she had birthed twins. Magda was jealous of her sister's love for Zmey and the fact she was the queen instead of Magda. So, she left Zunitza, not caring if she died, and abandoned the child in the demon forest hoping she would be torn apart.

"But that was me, and I wasn't killed," Diva said. "So how was I saved?"

Ula took a deep breath. "Drakus saved you and left you with Kosara. And you know the rest. Kosara brought you to Bendis, who asked us to raise you."

"It was all out of jealousy?" Diva snorted. "Both of them. Magda and Lamia. Jealous of Zmey and Zunitza. Do you have this kind of stuff happen in the human world?"

Pavel spoke before Theo could. "All the time. Life can be a real soap opera sometimes."

"Soap opera?" Diva waved her hand. "Never mind. So, how did I end up here after being in the castle?"

Theo cringed at the memories Ula unfolded for Diva. It had been difficult enough watching her get stabbed, without having to relive it again. Ula then told Diva about the ritual that had partially succeeded.

"So that must have been when I went wandering in the Forest of Souls," Diva said. "But you said it didn't bring me back all the way, so there's more to the story."

Ula nodded. "That's thanks to Theo. I'll let him tell you the rest."

Theo recounted everything that had happened since the ritual by the lake. When he finished, he let out a long breath.

Diva stared at him for a while before saying, "That's amazing. I'm glad you fought so hard for me." She paused and grinned. "Brother." With that, she wrapped her arms around him and gave him a bear hug.

When she finally let go, he was smiling, glad she was happy to have him for a brother.

Next, Diva turned and gave Pavel a big hug. "And thank you for being here with me the whole time."

Pavel's face turned red. "Uh, well, someone had to stay and help Ula."

Ula nodded and smiled as she came closer and wrapped her arms around Diva. "We're all so happy to have you back with us."

When everyone had finished hugging each other, Theo asked, "Why would Magda want my medallion, though?" He explained again how the vulture had tried to take it and also how Magda had shown an interest in the medallion once before. "She said that it's a twin gift. Mine had belonged to Zunitza. Magda also told me twin gifts have even more power when combined."

Ula shrugged. "I wouldn't know. Magda may be the only person who can tell us."

"Or Zunitza." Baba Yaga cackled.

Theo turned to look at the witch. "What do you mean?"

"I got the truth out of your aunt while you were fighting the vulture."

"And …?" Theo held his hands out palms up toward the witch. *Why does she have to always play games? Is she that desperate to be the center of attention?*

"Aaaaand …" Baba Yaga stretched out the word. "Not sure I should tell ya."

Ula gave the witch a stern look. "Baba Yaga."

"Oh, all right. Magda said she and Zunitza hid something special in their secret hiding spot."

"What does that have to do with my medallion?" Theo asked.

"Magda needs both yours and hers to open it."

Theo shook his head. "What can be so important to her that she'd send a vulture after me to get it?"

"Zunitza's crown."

Theo opened his eyes wide. "The one she was wearing at the fortress wasn't my mother's?"

Ula shook her head. "No. I grabbed that one when we took Diva away, thinking the same thing. It was just a cheap imitation. We can't let her get the actual crown. That, too, has great power."

Theo looked back at Baba Yaga. "Since the two of you were chatting like old friends, did Magda say where this hiding place was?"

"Nope."

"Nope she didn't say, or nope you're not going to tell us?"

"Didn't say."

"I'll find out from Zunitza later," Theo said. "How'd you manage to get all that information from her anyway?"

"I have my ways." The witch tapped her head. "They don't call me the witch of witches for nothing."

Theo groaned and turned away. "We should return to the castle and help Zmey plan the battle." He stopped and twisted back to look at Baba Yaga. "I forgot all about the Golden Apple. Did Magda have it? Did you get it from her?" Maybe they could avoid a battle. Diva was back and if—

Baba Yaga shook her head. "Nope."

Theo's distrust of the witch grew again. Did she actually have the apple, but had hidden it away? She loved gold and power. Was she thinking—?

"I see that look on your face." Baba Yaga rose, grunting with the effort. "I don't have the Golden Apple, and I didn't hide it."

Theo got up and paced the room. "If Magda still has the apple, we have a chance to get it back before she gives it to Lamia. But first, we have to hurry and let Zmey know everything that's happened."

Chapter 10
The Power of Light

JULY 14

THE SUN HAD RISEN while they'd filled in Diva on the highlights of everything that had happened. Theo basked in the glorious warmth as he soared toward the castle. He chose to fly as a dragon, rather than on Shar, to offer everyone greater protection if they ran into trouble along the way. The others rode on their deer. He hadn't slept all night, and neither had Pavel or Ula, apparently, but Theo felt refreshed. Diva was back in the land of the living, and she was ready to kick butt. He was thankful Baba Yaga had returned to her chicken hut. He'd had enough of being around the witch, and she wanted no part of battle planning.

At the castle, Theo led them through the passageway behind the ballroom to where everyone had gathered. He didn't tell his friends, especially Diva, that his father and others were meeting in a hidden library. Theo wanted to see Diva's expression when she beheld all the books, ones she thought had been lost forever when Lamia burned Jabalaka's house and the books he had there. Jabalaka had told Theo that those books were copies. The secret library housed the originals.

Outside the library door, Theo stopped. He grasped Diva's hand. "Are you ready?"

It would be her first time meeting Zmey with the knowledge that she was his daughter, as well as a princess. Theo recalled when he'd first met the dragon king after the curse that made him a statue had been broken. Theo had been super nervous, wondering how he should approach the ruler of Zmeykovo. But Zmey had welcomed Theo with open arms, literally. It had been a bitter-sweet moment. He had one of his birth parents, but he never had the opportunity to meet his mother, Zunitza, in the flesh, except for within his mind. He had longed to feel her embrace as well in this world.

Does Diva feel the same?

Her hand in his trembled slightly, and Theo gave it a squeeze.

She nodded, for once unable to voice words to her thoughts, Theo imagined.

"We'll all be right here with you," he said. "Me. Pavel. Ula."

Theo opened the door, wrapped his arm around Diva's shoulders, and stepped into the library.

Low voices hummed from every corner as the occupants prepared for battle. They found Zmey and the Colobari with their heads bowed over a table on which numerous scrolls had been laid out. The Samodivi, Kukeri, and Sitara held similar positions throughout the room. Theo assumed Drakus would arrive later in the afternoon.

Theo snuck a look at Diva. Her eyes were wide and her mouth slightly open as she swiveled her head, looking at shelves of books everywhere.

"They're all here." He nudged her. "All the books we thought Lamia had destroyed. They were copies. Zmeykovo's history hasn't been lost."

Tears threatened to flow from Diva's eyes. "It's … it's marvelous."

On her other side, Pavel took her free hand and squeezed it tight. "What a day this has been."

Sly came hopping out of the smaller room at that moment with Jabalaka right behind him. "Master, where do you want these—?"

Diva and Pavel both screamed, "You're alive!"

The hum in the room ceased. All eyes turned in the direction of the door. Once more, chaos broke out in the library, with everyone shouting and running around. This time, the sounds were those of joy.

A throng of people rushed toward Diva. Zmey stood dazed for a moment before he dropped the scroll he held and strode through the crowd. They parted for him, and he stood in front of Diva, his arms wide. Unshed tears brimmed his eyes, which were filled with boundless pain and love.

"Come, my daughter. My lost part of Zunitza. I'm so sorry I never knew."

Theo gave Diva a gentle push toward Zmey, who embraced her. A sense of relief flooded Theo that his sister was safe in the arms of their father. The only thing that would have made their family complete would be to have Zunitza with them in the flesh, but Theo was content that he at least had his mother's spirit with him.

Zmey smiled at Theo. "Thank you for believing in Zunitza's robe. But more importantly, thank you for bringing my daughter, your sister, back to us."

Ula stepped away from the commotion and spoke with Sava. The elder Samodiva sister nodded and looked around the room. She made her way toward Sitara, talked with him for a while. He spoke and pointed at papers he'd been reviewing. Sava said something again, and Sitara shrugged, but then he nodded and left the room.

Zmey released Diva and led her toward the Colobari, the only ones in the room who had remained at the table during all the commotion. The wizards bowed to him—or perhaps to Diva—as the two approached.

Theo and Pavel followed behind. Pavel had remained quiet during the reunion. His face showed both happiness and sorrow Theo thought.

"You're not going to lose her now that we got her back, you know," Theo said.

"Yah, I suppose not." Pavel shrugged. "But it's going to be different, like it was when you …"

Theo was sure Pavel was referring to the difficulties they'd had since Theo had discovered his magical roots and become the so-called hero of Zmeykovo. It had switched their roles. Pavel had always been the golden boy in their village of Selo, and Theo had been the one in the background.

All that had changed during their adventures in this land. Pavel felt like an uninvited guest, the odd one out in this land filled with magic. Diva had treated Pavel no differently than she had everyone else. The two of them had formed a unique friendship.

Pavel had once feared that Theo wouldn't need him any longer and was afraid their friendship would end. Now, Pavel must think the same thing about Diva.

Theo stopped walking and grasped Pavel's shoulders. "I never stopped being your friend. Everything I did was to try to protect you. Diva isn't going to change, either. All three of us will still be the best of friends."

Pavel sighed. "I hope so. I know I'm only human, but …"

"Neither of us is going to stop liking you. We're your friends because of who you are inside. It doesn't matter if you're human or dragon or nymph or witch …" Theo stopped and laughed. "Well, I might not like you if you were a witch like Baba Yaga."

That brought a grin to Pavel's face. "I guess. Time will tell."

"C'mon." Theo nodded toward where Diva stood with Zmey. "Let's drag her away from my father's planning and come up with ideas of our own. I'm sure we could use one of your inventions for the battle ahead."

They caught the tail end of the conversation Zmey was having with the Colobari. "So, we're all agreed that we'll perform the purification ritual on the Golden Apple when we get it back, since we no longer need it for healing?"

All three men bowed their heads.

Kobur the Eagle, as that was how Theo thought about the man since he was the Colobar who had emerged from the golden eagle statue, said, "That is the wisest choice. Rattan, locate the *Lodge of Light and Lodge of Darkness* so we can make ready for the ritual."

Rattan the Hawk nodded and stepped away.

Theo cleared his throat. "Jabalaka loaned that book to me so I could find out more about the Golden Apple. I was looking for a way to defeat Lamia."

Rattan raised his eyebrows. "And you understood the words?"

"Not all of them, but I read through much of the history."

"So not the rituals and incantations." A relieved look crossed the hawk-man's face.

"No, none of those." Theo smiled, hoping to further reassure Rattan. "I'll go get the book and be back in a moment."

He scrambled out of the library and back to his room, where he retrieved a book with a dark-red, cracked cover from under his pillow. Moments later, he returned and handed the heavy tome to Rattan.

The hawk-man nodded his thanks and turned to walk away.

"Would it be possible for us"—Theo pointed to himself, Pavel, and Diva—"to ask you questions. Not what the ritual is," he hurried to say, "but about how we can defeat Zlo. Magda told me that the Colobari predict when it's favorable to go to battle."

"Come." Rattan gestured toward a table away from the others.

As he set the book down, Diva skimmed over the books on a shelf. She ran her fingers along their spines and took deep breaths. Theo knew where she'd be spending much of her time after they defeated their enemies.

Pavel, on the other hand, opened the *Lodge* book, peering into its yellowed pages. "Wow, this is really old." Before Rattan could comment, Pavel added, "Don't worry. I can't read any of this. Does it talk about inventions? It might give me a clue what I can do to help."

"Inventions?" Rattan stepped away, looking at books. He pulled one out and brought it back to Pavel. "This has illustrations and is a language you'll understand."

"Way cool!" Pavel took the book and slid to the floor.

Diva, too, had found something of interest, and she joined Pavel.

With both his friends lost in books, Theo had Rattan to himself to find out how best to defeat Zlo. The Colobar gazed at Theo with knowing, yet curious eyes. The look was not so penetrating this time, as if the man had accepted that Theo posed no threat to the well-being of the kingdom or the sacred rites of the priesthood.

"What is it you wish to understand?" Rattan asked.

"I was wondering about Tangra's light," Theo started. "I know he's the Thracian god of the sun. I also was told the Zmeykovo deities cannot get directly involved in our affairs."

"Yes, this is true." The hawk-man nodded. "The Colobari determine Tangra's will and seek his guidance. We especially invoke his power in times of war and during other challenges as he embodies strength, courage, and honor."

"I was wondering how I can effectively harness his power, too."

Theo told Rattan about how Bendis had enhanced the power of his sword, not only with strengths she and the Firebird possessed, but also that she had granted him the use of Tangra's power.

"But," he added, "I keep hearing, 'He who has light within himself will tear apart the darkness.' Even with Tangra's light, every time I've fought Zlo, I've only been able to harm him when he is in solid form. The sword's power has had no effect when he changes into a black mist. So, how can I tear apart the darkness?"

"Wise observations," Rattan said. "But you must use more than the sword. You must become like the Colobari, the servants of Light, to defeat the servants of Darkness."

"And how do I do that?" Theo hoped the man wouldn't give him another riddle, but he braced himself for one.

"I understand your frustration with our ways." Rattan smiled. "I'll try to make it simple so you understand. If it's dark, and I want to read a book, I can light a candle and place it in front of the book. However, that will illuminate only my book. Correct?"

"Right." Theo nodded.

"That is Darkness. It allows you only small glimpses of what it is. When you focus the light on the book, that is all you see."

"Okay." Theo wasn't sure where this was going. He couldn't understand how reading a book would help him defeat Zlo, unless that book was the *Lodge of Light and Lodge of Darkness*. "So, are you saying the book is like Zlo's material form?"

"In a way," the hawk-man said. "Now think about what Light is. When I take that same candle and move it away from the book, it illuminates more of the room. The book as well as the darkness behind the book are both revealed."

"Yeeees." It still wasn't clear to Theo.

"One candle is not enough," Rattan continued. "If I surround the room with candles, the entire room is revealed, and the darkness is dispelled."

Theo thought about that. Bendis had given him three powers: Tangra's light, the Firebird's fire, and her power of the moon. All three were lights with different capabilities and intensities. He had used only one at a time. To defeat Zlo, he had to use all of them at once.

"Ah, I see you are beginning to comprehend," Rattan said. "But the power of others alone is not enough. To light a candle or more in a room is to use the light for yourself. To truly overcome Darkness, you must shine the Light for others."

Theo thought back to when Bendis bestowed the powers on his sword. More than the sword had glowed. The light had traveled over Theo's entire body.

With wide eyes, he looked at Rattan. "So, I must become the light, the flame, and surround the darkness?"

"Yes, Young Dragon Prince." The hawk man gave a small bow of his head. "Now I must ensure we can neutralize the Golden Apple." He opened the book Theo had brought and searched its contents.

Theo slid down the wall and sat with Diva and Pavel. "I don't want to interrupt your reading, but I think we should go back out and try to find Magda. If we can get the Golden Apple from her before she gives it to Lamia, if she hasn't already, we can prevent this war."

Pavel looked up. His eyes held a glazed look that Theo recognized as a sign that Pavel was devising a new invention in his mind. Pavel blinked, and his eyes cleared.

"We don't know if she even has it, though," he said.

"True, but we don't know that she doesn't either."

Diva closed her book. "Let's go. I don't think we'll accomplish much here. Let's plan our own strategy while we look for your aunt."

"She's your aunt now, too." Theo grinned.

"Okay," Pavel said. "But I want to make something first, in case we find her. You know how she can shift into different animals. What I have in mind will keep her trapped."

"Do we really have time for—?" Theo started, but Diva poked his side. "Uh, sure. It'll be good to be prepared."

"Great. I need—"

"My King! My King!" Sly burst into the room, his bulgy eyes swiveling around until he found Theo. He hopped over. "Witch is coming! So bad, so bad. You must see her."

Theo jumped up. "What's happening, Sly?"

"No, no. Sly cannot say. Bad punishment if Sly tell my King."

Theo sighed. *Just what I need. More promises Sly can't tell me about. And now I have to deal with Baba Yaga again.* At least he hoped the witch Sly had mentioned was Baba Yaga.

Chapter 11
Danger in the Woods

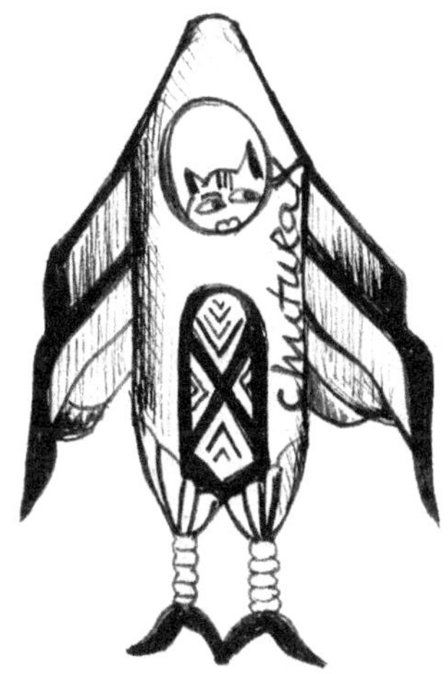

THEO, PAVEL, AND DIVA waited outside the castle for Baba Yaga's arrival. Instead of a mortar polluting the sky with black puffs of smoke, a shining, spinning object jetted toward them. It emitted strange thunderous noises.

Theo held his hand to his forehead to block out the morning sun's blinding rays. "Is that Baba Yaga? What happened to her decrepit old Chutura?"

As the flying object drew nearer, Diva said, "Yes, that's her. I can see her waving."

The noise intensified, like a revving engine, and Theo covered his ears. Baba Yaga adjusted flaps and moved levers as she hovered overhead like a helicopter. The mortar—if that was what this contraction was—made a jerky descent, speeding up and slowing down the way a car moved when an inexperienced driver overused the brakes. The vehicle screeched and gears made a sickening grinding sound as two wheels shot out from the bottom.

The mortar landed with a *thud*, spewing up dirt and rocks. After a few moments, the noise blessedly stopped, and the dust storm subsided.

Kotka, with her fur standing on end, hissed as she flew out from the inside of the flying device. The cat circled overhead, snarling and growling as if warding off a potential rival.

Coughing, Baba Yaga hobbled out next on wobbly legs. "Well, that will take some getting used to. Not too bad for only my second flight. At least this time, it landed upright and not on top of anyone's head."

"What *is* this thing?" Theo came closer to inspect the flying vessel. It was golden with so many gears and levers that it was no wonder the witch had trouble flying it. "What happened to your noisy, smoke-puffing Chutura?"

"Don't touch it!" Baba Yaga swatted Theo's hand. "This is my new, improved, state-of-the-art design. My new Chutura Pestle XSpace. It's fast, reliable, and has room to carry a friend. Courtesy of the Samodivi. They finally made good on their promise. They appreciated my help in rescuing their sister and went top of the line for me."

"Top of the line?" Pavel snorted. "I didn't think flying mortars came in more than one style. I think you're the only one who has ever flown one. It's way cool, though. Maybe you'll let me try it out?"

"Not on your life." Baba Yaga cackled. "Literally. You risk your life flying this thing."

Theo could think of only one person who could have come up with a solid gold mortar. "So, this is what Sava was talking to Sitara about?"

"Yep, yep, yep." Baba Yaga preened. "She's all mine. The blacksmith put the final touches on it today." She looked around. "We seem to be missing someone."

"Kotka flew off in a huff," Theo said.

"Oh, not her." The witch peered inside her new, improved Chutura. "Kiki? Kiki? You can come out now. We've landed."

Two goatlike horns poked out from the inside of the mortar, followed by a curved beak. Soon, bright, bulging eyes followed as Kikimora drew her head out and looked around.

Pavel gasped and jumped away from the mortar, stepping closer to Diva. He'd never gotten over the fact that Kikimora had tried to drag him into the swamp where she lived. None of them had ever asked her about it, so they remained mystified what her intent was. That, as well as the nightmares Pavel had suffered from Zima's curse, had left Pavel terrified of her ever since.

The scrawny, hunchbacked creature stood all the way up. Her headscarf lay askew, and her normally tangled hair was in even more disarray.

Kikimora chirped and placed her hand over her heart as she set her chicken legs outside of the mortar. "Oh, boy. I'm glad we survived." She turned to Baba Yaga. "I don't think using beer to propel your mortar was a good idea."

"Beer? He he, ho ho." Baba Yaga cackled. "No, no. My new Chutura runs on water and solar power. You, my dear, are the one who runs on beer."

"What brings you here, witch?" Theo asked. "Sly was insistent that I come see you about something that was so bad he couldn't tell me what it was."

"He he, ho ho. I'll let Kiki explain." Baba Yaga stepped aside.

Kikimora fluttered her eyelids at Theo. "Hello, handsome boy. My Lesnik has returned, and he wants to speak with you."

Theo couldn't believe it. Lesnik still thought he deserved something after making Theo chase him around Zmeykovo. "I'm not bringing him beer. He didn't do enough to deserve a reward. And he and his friend, Lord Vodnik, had enough of that brew already."

Kikimora let out a long chirp and looked at Theo with her big eyes. "My Les says it's important. He overheard Magda and—"

"Magda!" Theo now paid attention. "Lesnik knows where my aunt is?"

"That's what she's been trying to tell ya, if you'd listen," Baba Yaga said.

Theo glared at the witch, but then turned back to Kikimora. "Is he still at your place? I'll go there right away."

"Oh, no." Sadness crossed Kikimora's face. "He grabbed beer and said to go where you first met him. He was scared, my Les. Please help him. For me?"

Theo's heart melted. Kikimora had cured him of Lamia's possession, and the swamp creature genuinely seemed to care about him. Even though he thought she was too good for Lesnik, he would help her if it meant she'd be happy.

"All right. I'll do it. We need to find my aunt."

Kikimora chirped again. "Thank you, my handsome boy."

"Okay, Kiki," Baba Yaga said, "Our job here is done. Let's get you back home."

They climbed into the new Chutura. Kiki fluttered her eyes once more at Theo as Baba Yaga adjusted gears and took off into the sky like a golden arrow.

Pavel let out a long breath. "Glad to see the last of them. But if we're going to try to find Magda, I need to make a new invention that I saw in the book Rattan gave me."

"I don't think we have time," Theo said.

"Trust me," Pavel replied. "I'm sure it'll work the way it has in the past right here in Zmeykovo. And the best part is, the invention mostly already exists. I saw one in the treasure room when you brought Baba Yaga there. I just need to make a few modifications."

Theo silently groaned. Who knew what kind of modifications it needed and how long it would take.

"Don't give me that look." Pavel scowled. "This *will* work."

"Okay, okay. Let's go to the treasure room."

BACK INSIDE THE CASTLE after Pavel found what he needed, he dumped the contents from his backpack onto his bed. He spread them out next to the silver net he'd retrieved from the treasure room. The threads were thin, but strong.

Pavel sighed as he looked wistfully at the schematic for his Dracophone that he'd started to build.

"Do you really want to use those parts?" Theo asked. "I thought you were trying to find a way to call home."

Pavel shrugged. "I have a feeling we'll be able to go there soon. Back in Selo, I have better parts I can use to make another phone that might actually work."

Theo felt bad. Pavel's inventions didn't always work, but he put so much energy into building them that it seemed a shame to dismantle one before he even had a chance to try it.

"Besides," Pavel added, "capturing Magda is more important at the moment."

He nimbly took the device apart and added pieces around the netting, which he then folded into a tiny square. Around it, he wrapped a tube. When he finished, the device looked like a flashlight.

"There, done. The book calls this a Telkapan, a wire trap. People threw it over demons, but I've modified it so when I press this button, it'll eject the net about twenty feet into the air. The book says that the silver the net is made from will prevent demons from escaping."

"It seems so fragile." Theo shook his head.

"This type of material is made by the Rusalki," Diva said, "and they've used these nets to capture bigger prey than Magda."

Pavel scooped the unused parts back into his backpack. "Don't worry. It'll work. Let's go see what Lesnik has to say."

The trio left the castle and called their deer. As they flew to Zmeykovo's dragon tail, Theo felt mixed emotions. He was worried Lesnik might be playing tricks again or, worse, leading Theo and his friends into a trap. But what would Lesnik's motive be? He'd already taken beer from his neglected wife and deserted her again. Even though it might be a trap, Theo was elated, too, about the trip. This time, he was having an adventure with the two people he trusted most.

They landed by the hideaway in a short time. Theo slid off of his deer companion and called out, "Lesnik, I'm here. Don't play any games this time. We have to find Magda."

Pavel grabbed hold of Theo's arm. "That tree ... it's moving!"

Theo looked. It was true. A tree approached them. With each step—for Theo couldn't think of how else to describe the movement of the roots—the tree shrank. Its branches waved and morphed into arms and the leaves into hands, while the roots took on the shape of legs and feet. By the time the walking tree had reached them, it had changed into a leaf-covered man.

"No games." Lesnik glanced all around them. "I had to have you come here because one of Lord Vodnik's children kept following me. Around the marsh. To Kiki's house. Everywhere. He kept those buggy eyes looking at me."

"That was probably Sly," Theo said. "He's not Lord Vodnik's spy. That creature terrifies Sly. It's quite the opposite. Sly lets Jabalaka know what's going on and was the one who told us Baba Yaga was coming. So out with it. What's got you scared? What did Magda say?"

Lesnik crept closer and whispered, "They thought I was asleep, but I overheard Lord Vodnik agree to help her."

"How?" Diva poked the forest guardian in the chest. "I'll know if you're lying."

"Magda is going to make a drowning spell." Lesnik darted his eyes around the forest again. "When you all come to the fortress to attack her, she's going to fill the area with a mist."

Pavel snorted. "You can't drown in a mist."

"This one you can." Lesnik nodded vigorously. "Water creatures like Lord Vodnik can create suffocating water. They thicken water until a person can't move."

Theo shivered remembering when he and Diva had been looking for Jabalaka in the Cold Marsh. A Vodnik had pulled Theo under the water and had almost drowned him in that suffocating water. He had no doubt that Magda could do what she planned with Lord Vodnik's help.

"Anything else?" Theo asked.

Lesnik shook his head.

"We thank you for your help," Theo told him.

With another glance around the forest, Lesnik slunk away, shrinking to the size of a blade of grass as he made his way back to his former hiding spot.

"I smell a trap," Pavel said. "Isn't he good buddies with Lord Vodnik? Why would he willingly tell us all this, unless he wanted to trick us?"

Theo sent out his dragon senses to scan the forest near them. Something did feel off, like a predator waiting to pounce on unsuspecting prey. He put his finger to his lips to let Diva and Pavel know to be quiet. Theo searched farther with his eyes and ears. Only one threat was nearby. Whatever was out there was biding its time.

"*Do you think it's waiting for a signal from Lesnik?*" he thought to his friends.

He was glad that Pavel could now understand thought-talk. Theo wanted to keep his friend aware of what was going on, even when none of them could speak.

Pavel shrugged, but Diva thought back, "*I don't think he's involved. He was sincere about what he said.*"

"*So someone followed us?*" Pavel thought. "*But how? I didn't see anyone behind us in the air.*"

"*Or someone was already here,*" Diva thought.

"*Magda?*" they all thought at the same time.

The deer became jittery moments before a black wolf growled and leapt out of the forest.

Theo ducked and rolled, narrowly missing being mauled by the animal's sharp claws. He whipped his sword out of its sheath and stood with legs bent and arms extended, ready to battle the beast. Pavel had scrambled out of the way, and Diva held her bow with arrow nocked.

The black wolf crouched as if ready to pounce again. Its eyes glowed red like hot coals, its fur bristled, and its pointed teeth dripped with bloody saliva. The animal snarled as it crept closer. It lunged again, fangs bared. Theo dodged the attack, swinging his sword at the beast but missing.

Diva's aim was truer. Her arrow found its mark in the wolf's side, causing the animal to yelp. Seeing his chance, Theo plunged his sword into the wolf's flank. The beast howled and thrashed, trying to dislodge the weapons. Theo clung on, thrusting the sword deeper.

The wolf writhed, and its body began to shrink like air leaking from a tire. Fur transformed into feathers, and a maw into a beak. The sword and arrow fell free.

Where the wolf had been, a black crow now struggled to flap its wings.

"We can't let it get away," Pavel shouted.

He ran toward the crow and aimed his Telkapan. The bird took flight, floundering in the air as it tried to gain height. Pavel pressed the button on his invention, and the silver net shot out. The crow cawed as it became entangled within the fibers. It clawed and shrieked to no avail, dropping like a deadweight to the ground.

"What do we do with it now?" Pavel asked. "We lost our chance to capture Magda."

"Maybe not." Diva kneeled by the thrashing crow. "Look."

Tattooed on the bird's wing was a seven-pointed star symbol like Theo's medallion.

"Yes, that's Magda, all right." Theo smiled and turned to Pavel. "Great job! Let's get back to the castle and let Zmey know we have a prisoner."

Chapter 12
Prisoner

THE GOLDEN RAYS of the sun dipped behind Cherna Mountain as Theo and his friends neared the castle. He gripped the struggling crow against his chest. She beat her wings and pecked at the silver strands of the net. Theo squeezed her tighter. He was determined that this time Magda wasn't going to escape. They needed answers from her, and she had to pay for her crimes against her family.

After landing outside the gate, he, Pavel, and Diva thanked their deer companions, and the animals returned to the herd. A guard let the trio pass through the heavy gates. In the courtyard, Zmey paced at the top of the marble steps leading into the castle. Several warriors surrounded him.

"There you are." The dragon king sighed with relief as the three of them scrambled up the steps. "No one could tell me where you'd gone."

"Sly didn't stay in the library?" Theo asked. "He's the one who dragged us away."

"No, no one had a clue where you were."

Theo hoped Sly was okay. The Vodnik had been so terrified that he'd be punished if he said anything against his father.

"Maybe he went back to do more spying," Pavel said.

"Could be." Theo remembered how Jabalaka had said Sly was his eyes and ears to what was happening in Zmeykovo. "Anyway, we have a prisoner I think you'll want to interrogate."

"A prisoner?" Zmey scanned around them. "Where?"

"Here." Theo held up the struggling crow. "Magda."

He recounted to Zmey their latest adventure, Magda's attack, and how Pavel had caught the crow with his modified invention.

Zmey gestured to two of his warriors. "Lock her up in the cell in Zandan where Lamia kept the Samodivi prisoners. We'll join you shortly to question her."

One man took the flailing bundle in the net, and the two warriors disappeared into the castle. Theo was glad Zmey had suggested that cell in the prison. It was fortified so magical creatures couldn't escape.

"I'll inform the Colobari of Magda's capture," Zmey said. "Then we can see what she can or will tell us."

"You should also know about another treachery." Theo recounted how they'd left because of an urgent message from Lesnik. "Lord Vodnik is helping Magda create a new form of suffocating water."

Zmey sighed. "He's always been a thorn in my side. We'll deal with him after we stop Lamia and Zlo. At least with Magda now captive, that puts an end to their plans."

They followed Zmey to the library and waited outside while the dragon king spoke with the wizards, or priests as Theo preferred to think of them, since the men served the sun god, Tangra. When Zmey returned, the group proceeded down a hallway, going deeper into the underground portion of the castle. Diva and Pavel huddled in the middle, softly conversing, while Theo took up the rear. Their footsteps echoed down the stone passageways. Only an occasional torch lit the way, possibly ignited by the soldiers who had been sent on ahead with Magda. The flickering light cast eerie shadows that danced across the ground.

Theo and his friends had been to the prison once before on his first visit to Zmeykovo. They had snuck into the castle through tunnels and ended up in the torture room. From there, they hid in barrels that had held rotten food that was served to the prisoners. Strange beasts had loaded those barrels onto carts, which then traveled an outside route to the castle. This time, making his way to the prison through the twists and turns of the castle tunnels proved to be just as smelly a route.

Pavel must have had the same thought because he scrunched up his nose. "It smells like Kikimora's house, but some foul new brand of beer that she's brewing. The air down here is also so musty and damp." Pavel plucked at his shirt as the sweat dripped down his face and neck.

Worse than either of those, Theo thought.

The darkness seemed to be pressing down on him. It felt as if he were entering the mouth of a beast, like returning to Devil's Throat. His second trip there had been more overwhelming than the first, since Theo's dragon abilities had developed. Sights, sounds, smells, even feelings … all were enhanced.

Despite the heat, a coldness grazed Theo's neck, and something tugged at his medallion. He grasped the chain, which he'd fixed earlier, and swung around, searching for the culprit, but found nothing. His heart pounded. Something sinister clung to the air. Theo could sense invisible eyes fixated on him.

The intense feeling followed him to the enchanted prison cells. No one had to tell Theo they had arrived. Magic bristled all around.

A soldier stood on either side of a metal door. At Zmey's command, one of the men unbolted the entrance to the cell and opened it. Metal scraped against stone, making a screeching noise worthy of a horror movie.

The dragon king gestured to Theo, Diva, and Pavel. "Follow me."

"Do you think Magda's still in there?" Pavel whispered to Theo. "She has the power to change into anything."

Theo's heart raced. Near total darkness filled the room. Even so, it *did* appear to be empty. Had his aunt turned herself into an insect?

But then, Zmey walked to the opposite wall, where he moved aside pitch-black curtains to reveal another room surrounded by silver bars set into the stone. A metal cage chained to the wall sat in the middle of the cell. Inside the cage, the crow, still wrapped tight in the net, beat her wings and scratched her claws against her prison.

Zmey lit a torch in a sconce. "It's time to have a talk, Magda."

The crow's eyes burned red while she struggled against her confinement. As Zmey drew nearer, she fought harder to escape, emitting shrill screams. Theo's dragon senses picked out an occasional defamatory word or curse his aunt thought about both of his parents

Zmey must have heard them, too, for he said, "Now, now, no need for such language. You've brought this all on yourself. We'll be able to talk normally once I remove the magical net from you."

"No, don't!" Pavel backed against the wall. "She'll turn into a snake or that black mist and escape."

The dragon king stopped mid-stride and turned his head toward Pavel. "Her magic won't allow her to escape from this room. Like your net, the bars are made of silver and powerful enchantments. Magda won't be able to get through them."

Diva nodded. "It's true. My sisters tried everything they could think of to escape from this room when Lamia had imprisoned them. All their efforts failed."

Theo moved to block the doorway, just in case. He didn't trust his aunt. She was certain to try some sort of trickery. If she got too close to the exit, he wouldn't let her escape.

Zmey opened the cage door and lifted the net from Magda. She flew in a rage at him, but he grasped her by the neck, holding her at eye level. "None of that. I'll release you, so you can speak. My children have weapons that can defeat you, so refrain from your tricks."

Zmey let go of the crow. Feathers dissolved into a funnel of black smoke, and reshaped into Magda's form. She slunk to the corner and fiddled with her bracelet. Once more she changed shape, turning into a black snake that slithered across the floor toward the exit with the speed of the wind. Theo braced himself to step on her, but an arrow pierced the snake's tail, binding it to the stone. The creature twisted and turned until it freed itself. With another puff of smoke, Magda returned to her Samodiva form. Hatred and bitter rage seared her face.

Zmey stepped closer. "It's time to be civil. We were friends once, and Zunitza loved you so much. Try to remember that before you spew out any more of your hate. You still have the opportunity to be part of our family if you mend your ways."

"You were never my friend or family." Magda snarled as her hand fiddled with a chain around her neck. "I hated Zunitza. She had everything that should have been mine. The crown. The love of the people. A family. I was her shadow. No one ever saw me, respected me. You and my sister were always out to deprive me of my destiny. I was born to rule."

A sad smile flitted across Zmey's lips. "Love trumps destiny."

"Love! What you shared with Zunitza was not love." Magda's eyes turned a fiery red. "It was greed. Lust. A desire for power. My sister was no better than I was. She thought she was destined to be Zmeykovo's heroine."

Theo's heart raced. The first time Magda had mentioned that the medallion he wore was Zunitza's twin gift, he'd wondered if the prophecies were about her rather than him. His mother had thought that, too. Yet, she had given the medallion to him, to protect him since she couldn't be there to do that in the human world. He choked back a sob. Had giving him her medallion sealed her fate and cost her her life?

"Enough!" Zmey's eyes hardened, and his knuckles turned white as he tightened his grip. "You've hurt my family enough with your lies, actions, and accusations. Worse than keeping from me and Zunitza the fact that we had a daughter was your attempt to kill Diva. It's time for all of that evil behavior to stop. Redeem yourself before you become as crazed as my sister, if you haven't already. Give us the Golden Apple, so we can restore order."

Hysterical laughter erupted from Magda, and her body shook. Her eyes glinted with malice. "You're too late. I've already taken it to Lamia in exchange for becoming the queen of the Samodivi and Youdi, and even the Rusalki. That title belongs to me from birth."

"But Lamia tried to kill you," Pavel spluttered from his position against the wall. "How can you trust her?"

"Indeed." Zmey nodded. "Do you really think she'll share any power with you? She is nothing but Zlo's puppet. It is through Lamia that he intends to rule over all of Zmeykovo. My sister can only promise what he's allowed her to say. And it's all lies."

Theo sucked in a deep breath. He thought about the times Lamia had tried to sway him over to her side, saying she wanted to defeat Zlo. Theo had always thought her pleas were trickery, but maybe she'd found moments or places where she could escape Zlo's influence. Perhaps there had been some truth in her words.

Something else niggled in his brain. Lamia's hatred of Zmey. Even if she wanted to throw off Zlo's yoke, Lamia still despised her brother. Was that Zlo's influence, as well? Or had something else caused that anger to poison her blood?

"You're the one who lies!" Magda shouted. "Once I get the crown …" She slapped her hand over her mouth.

Theo approached his aunt. "We already know that's why you want my medallion. Baba Yaga told us about the crown's power and the secret hiding place. You can't open it without both your medallion and mine."

"And neither can you." Magda sneered at Theo. "If I can't be queen, then no one will. And I'll never tell you where the hiding place is."

"You don't have to. I can ask my mother." Theo walked closer, standing next to Zmey. "If you both had to be present to unlock your hiding place, I don't understand why my mother would have hidden it there. Why would she have allowed you to know where it was?"

A wicked grin spread across Magda's face. "It wasn't me she tried to hide it from. It was Lamia. After she returned from the human world, having hidden her other precious possession away—you!—she wanted to keep the crown's power away from Lamia. The only place she thought was safe enough was our secret niche."

Theo shook his head. "How could she trust you? You'd left her to die in the forest in Selo."

"Oh, she was easy to deceive." Magda sneered. "I told her I had gone to fetch special herbs to ease her pain in case the others didn't work, and when I returned to where I'd left her, she was no longer there."

Diva spoke up from the wall where she stood next to Pavel. "And you think she didn't see through your lies?"

Magda shrugged. "It doesn't matter what she thought. I suggested that she hide the crown there, and she agreed."

"Maybe she knew that it would be the only place that was safe from you," Diva said.

Fire flashed in Magda's eyes. "If that was true, then it was only safe while she was alive. I was there at her side when she died. When I couldn't find the medallion on her, I was enraged. I didn't know what she'd done with it until I saw Theo wearing it."

"Even if you ever get the crown, you won't be queen." Emotion choked Diva's voice. "Zunitza was the only one worthy of that title."

Pavel wrapped his arm around her waist. "And Diva will take her place one day, because she is just as worthy. She loves this land, unlike you."

"Be quiet, human boy." Magda twisted her bracelet again. "Or I'll turn you into a gecko."

Zmey turned toward the door. "If you don't have the apple and are unwilling to help us, we have no more time to waste on you. You'll remain here until Zmeykovo is safe again. I'll decide then what your fate will be."

Zmey gestured for Theo, Diva, and Pavel to leave. Pavel snatched up the silver net, then scrambled after the others. The dragon king closed and bolted the door behind him.

Magda pounded on the door. "Let me out! Give me the crown. It's mine. All of it belongs to me, even you!"

Her voice weakened as Theo followed his father and friends down the dimly lit corridor. A coldness slithered around Theo, and he shivered. His skin prickled with magic. Had some of Magda's essence clung to him when he left the cell?

Chapter 13
Secret Weapon

JULY 15

THE NEXT MORNING, Theo trudged his way down to the library. Alone. No one else had been around. Not Diva. Not Pavel. Theo was surprised that they hadn't waited for him.

Although he'd slept hard and long, he dragged his feet, finding it difficult to move. Not only did his body ache, his mind felt fuzzy, and his eyes were heavy. He couldn't shake off the chill he'd experienced in the prison. It was as if someone or something had marked him. This wasn't like the time Lamia had possessed him, though. This feeling was external. An evilness about it made his skin crawl. He'd felt this power once before, but couldn't place exactly where, although he knew that he should be able to.

When he reached the library, he leaned against the doorjamb. His breath came out in gasps. Inside was once more a bustle of activity. While waiting for his heart rate and breathing to return to normal, Theo scanned the room for Diva and Pavel. They huddled around a table with Zmey and the Colobari. After taking one more deep breath, Theo strode over to join them. He was determined to be part of the battle planning.

"There you are, sleepyhead," Pavel said. "You were sleeping the sleep of the dead. We tried everything to wake you."

Theo shrugged. "Yesterday was exhausting."

"Don't we all know it." Pavel snuck a glance at Diva. "Zmey would like us to get weapons and equipment Sitara's been forging all night."

Zmey looked up. "That's correct. Theo, I'd like you to fly there and back as a dragon. Diva and Pavel can make sure the supplies are secure on your back. This is a special batch. It's too risky to have carts travel up and down the mountain with these weapons."

"Of course," Theo said. "We'll go right away."

The trio traveled in silence to the courtyard. Theo closed his eyes for a moment, enjoying a light breeze and the warmth of the sun. It melted away the chill, although traces of the evil lurked, hiding from the light.

The courtyard was a bustle of activity. Carts laden with shields, spears, and other military paraphernalia rattled over cobblestones as the equipment was distributed to Zmey's remaining soldiers. Those who already had donned protective gear practiced fighting techniques. The morning sun glinted off the soldiers' shields and helmets.

Theo passed outside the castle's gates and shifted into dragon form. Diva and Pavel climbed onto his back, and Theo leapt into the air. Below him, lush green fields surrounded the castle, and the moat had been filled to the brim with water. It sparkled like diamonds in the sunlight. A blue, cloudless sky lay before him. Although the scene was idyllic, tension filled the air. The clashing of weapons and the marching of soldiers echoed as he left the safety of the castle grounds.

He swooped down the mountainside and in a short while arrived at Vida Village, where Sitara had his blacksmith shop. Theo landed in the meadow and shifted back to boy form. This area was the haunt of the enemy Youdi, whose fortress overlooked the village, so it was best for the three of them to proceed with caution.

They met no resistance as they walked to the smithy. The doors had been thrown wide open, and a heavy, sweltering heat from the forge wafted outside. Sparks flew around the room, and the smell of burning metal filled the air. On their previous visits, Sitara had only one apprentice, a young boy. Today, several men and women scurried about, forging new weapons and repairing old ones. Muscles bulged as people wielded hammers, shaping the hot metal.

"There he is." Pavel pointed to the back of the room where Sitara was inspecting a sword. His apprentice stood by the blacksmith's side, nodding at whatever instructions Sitara was providing. He handed the boy the sword, and the apprentice bowed and rushed away.

"I see you've gained lots of new students," Theo said as he approached.

Sitara turned their way. "No, still just the one. The others are here to help prepare for the approaching battle. You've come for the weapons we have ready, I assume."

All three of them nodded.

"Follow me." Sitara led them downstairs to the smaller room where the blacksmith had once told them he forged more delicate objects. And magical ones, too.

The room had been cleared of the gems and precious metals it had once held. In their place, swords, lances, shields, and an assortment of other objects of war lined the walls. Sitara's crossbow still hung in its lofty place. At least now, it wasn't a weapon meant to kill the blacksmith, since his Vurkolak curse had been cured.

Pavel skipped over to a large mold. "Wow, is this what you used to make Baba Yaga's new mortar? How'd you manage to get that done so quickly?"

"Yes, and I had already begun the mortar before Sava asked me to finish it."

"Maybe you could tell me how you put it all together?" Pavel gave the blacksmith a puppy-dog look.

Sitara laughed. "Perhaps. After life gets back to normal here. Right now, I need these special weapons transported back to Zmey."

Diva approached a sword and ran her hands along the hilt. "You've added magic to them."

"Something I learned from the Youdi."

Theo came closer and inspected a sword. Runes lined the blade. He'd seen weapons like this before in this room. He, too, could feel magic vibrating off of them. "Aren't these the ones you made for the Youdi?"

Sitara shook his head. "No. They've already collected theirs, but they're in for a surprise. The weapons won't do what they expect them to."

"Why is that?" Diva asked. "This is powerful magic."

Sitara leaned closer and whispered, "I lined their runes with silver. The metal will counteract the magic when they try to activate it."

Theo was glad Sitara was now on their side, Zmey's side, and putting his energy into saving Zmeykovo. Before the blacksmith had been cured, he'd held no love for the dragon king, believing that humans like him would be expelled from the land when they no longer served a purpose. After Baba Yaga cured Sitara, not only was his curse gone, but also the hatred and anger that had built up over the many years of his imprisonment.

"Let me get my apprentice to gather a few of the other helpers." Sitara laid his hand on Theo's shoulder, and it felt as if a hundred-pound rock had landed on him. "They'll bring the weapons out to the meadow, so you can transport them to Zmey."

When the blacksmith left, Pavel slid a silver helmet, decorated with dragon images, onto his head. It covered his face to below his glasses.

Theo laughed. "I think you need a kiddy-sized one. I wonder if Sitara would even have a mold that small."

"Ha ha, not funny." Pavel scowled.

"Pavel has a brave heart," Diva said in his defense. "I'm sure we can find something suitable for him to wear."

"I have just the thing." Sitara clomped down the stairs, with several men following.

He directed his helpers to gather up the weapons and to go to the meadow, where Theo, Diva, and Pavel would join them momentarily. Sitara then opened a cupboard and removed a smaller helmet and a short sword. Runes covered both.

"I know you don't have magic, being human like me, but these items will give you a little extra protection from those who do possess magic." Sitara handed the items to Pavel. "These runes will shoot back to the sender whatever evil intent is directed at you."

"Wow! Thanks so much." Pavel's face beamed.

"Now is there anything else I can do for you three before I forge more weapons?"

"No," they said in unison.

"Thank you, Sitara," Theo added. "With you on our side, we'll be certain to win this battle once and for all."

BACK AT THE CASTLE, Zmey distributed the magical weapons to his special guard, the few remaining Knights of Light who hadn't been corrupted or enchanted by Zlo's power. Then, Zmey, Theo, Diva, and Pavel returned to the library to continue strategizing about how to best defeat their enemies.

The Colobari had already gathered around a large table. They were deep in conversation as they pored over maps and charts. Their murmured whispers mingled with the shuffling of pages and the creaking of chairs.

Kobur the Eagle unfolded a leather map. Theo had seen a similar one when they'd attacked Kaleto Fortress once before. This map, however, contained greater detail. Besides displaying gates, towers, and the complex system of underground tunnels, it also included the mountainous terrain surrounding the fortress.

Pavel wormed his way toward the map. "Are you trying to figure out how to get in? We've tried a lot of different routes, so you'll have to discover a new one."

Theo peered over Pavel's shoulder. "Maybe we can find another place that has fewer guards like the first time, or even a weak spot where we can knock over the walls."

"No to both your suggestions." Kobur shook his head. "The fortress walls were built centuries ago to survive normal attacks, but we have a secret weapon."

"What?" Theo asked.

"The race that built the fortress. The Ispolini." Kobur pointed to markings sprinkled around the area.

Theo blinked. "But … but … I thought Hala turned them into stone." That was the tale Diva had told him and Pavel after they had stumbled across trees resembling fighting giants. Hala, Zmey and Lamia's mother, had lured the Ispolini to an area where she could defeat them: among the blackberries. The giants' feet became entangled within the thorns, and Hala cast her enchantment on them. Over the centuries, trees had grown around the stone giants.

"Indeed, she did."

"Then how—?"

Before Theo could finish the thought, Diva, her eyes wide and shining, whispered, "You can bring the Ispolini back?"

Diva had once said she wished she could have met the giants of old. Now, from the smile on Kobur's face, it appeared Diva and the rest of them were going to have that opportunity. But the stone giants they'd seen were far from Kaleto Fortress. They wouldn't appear on the map Kobur was examining. But another time, when Theo and his friends had traveled over rocky terrain to find a less-guarded entrance to Kaleto Fortress, they had encountered an area of jagged rocks that resembled grotesque, deformed monsters. At the time, Theo had wondered if they, too, were the Ispolini, but he had convinced himself that they were only figures carved from the wind and rain.

He looked at the map again and pointed to marked spots. "So, these really were … are the Ispolini?"

"Yes." Kobur nodded.

"But will they help us if you remove the enchantment?" Theo asked. "Aren't they the natural enemies of dragons?"

"Yah," Pavel said. "And I don't think I'd want to help an enemy who turned me to stone."

"And on top of that," Theo added, "if you can remove the enchantment, why wasn't it done before now?"

"Now that is quite the tale." Kobur smiled. "To be brief, however, I will tell you that in order to reverse what was done, circumstances have to mimic what the situation was when the enchantment was cast."

"And what were those circumstances?" Theo asked.

"First, Zmeykovo must be in a state of chaos," Kobur said, "which is typically the case whenever the Golden Apple is born."

Theo thought back to the book that documented the history of Zmeykovo as it related to the Golden Apple. Violence erupted all over the land each time the Znahar Tree bore a Golden Apple. So many individuals vied to possess the magical fruit. Those were bloody, violent times.

"And second, and this is why it has taken so long," Kobur added, "the Golden Apple has to be born outside of its normal thousand-year birth. This occurs when the Firebird has been slain."

"So, you're saying someone killed the Firebird around the time the Ispolini were at war with Hala?" Theo asked. "And, this is the first time since then that it's happened again?"

"Yes," Kobur said. "There is much more to the story, but we must make our plans if we wish to succeed."

Theo wanted to ask more about how they would awaken the Ispolini, but Kobur had turned away and was examining the map. Beside him, Zmey and the other two Colobari hunched over and began their murmuring again. Theo paced behind them. He still had questions. In particular, Kobur hadn't addressed the issue of whether or not the Ispolini would help their natural enemies, the dragons. Perhaps the priest didn't know.

Rattan the Hawk leaned toward Kobur and whispered. A nod came from the elder Colobar, or at least the one Theo thought must be their leader. Rattan stepped away from the table and approached Theo.

"Young Dragon Prince. And Young Dragon Princess. And Young Friend." With each address, the Colobar bowed his head. "Come with me. I will explain what you need to know."

They moved over to a table by the bookshelves.

Rattan looked at each of them. "I will tell you what I know of the Ispolini. They once lived in the human world. There, they were fearsome beings. Bloodthirsty and devourers of dragon flesh."

Theo cringed, imagining the giants taking on dragons. "Full dragons only? Or the human dragons, too?"

"Sadly, both," Rattan replied. "The ancient Thracian gods allowed the Ispolini to start to die out once their flaw of becoming entangled in blackberries became known. The deities deemed the giant race was unsuitable for life in the human world."

Pavel huffed. "That's rather harsh. I mean, I don't like that they ate dragons, but, gee, just because they had a problem with thorns is no reason to annihilate an entire race."

"That is what Bendis thought, too." Rattan nodded. "This all occurred around the time of a cataclysmic event in your world, one that simultaneously altered Zmeykovo. Our Great Goddess invited all mystical races to live here. She made the Ispolini promise to live in harmony with the others."

"And did they?" Theo asked.

"Yes." Rattan sighed. "They asked to be isolated from everyone, to live in the mountains. It was there that they began to till the soil. The once fearsome beings became gentle and aloof. All they wanted was their privacy."

Diva asked, "Do you think they'll help us fight Lamia and Zlo?"

"We hope they will," Rattan replied. "If not for Zmeykovo, at least to regain their land."

Theo hoped the Colobar was right. "Even if they don't, it's the right thing to do to bring them back. How can you be sure you can even do that if it's never been done before?"

Rattan peered deep into Theo's eyes. "You are correct. It has not been done before. Failure is possible, but we will do our best to reverse the enchantment. The *Lodge of Light and Lodge of Darkness* holds many mysteries. You must believe in the unbelievable."

Theo couldn't help but wonder why Jabalaka had let the book out of his sight and allowed Theo to read it. Perhaps because Theo couldn't understand the magical content? But how would Jabalaka have known that? The Keeper's belief in Theo must have been enormous to entrust that sacred book to someone not initiated into the sacred rites.

"Zmey, my king!" A soldier rushed into the room, shattering Theo's thoughts. "Magda has escaped!"

Chapter 14
Battle Plans

With great haste, Theo followed Zmey back to the cell where Magda had been held prisoner. Tagan the Falcon, the one Colobar who remained mysterious to Theo, accompanied them at Kobur the Eagle's command.

The cell door was wide open, and the soldiers who had been guarding her lay dead on the ground, their throats torn out as if a wild animal had attacked them. Theo wanted to vomit, and he couldn't think straight. He was glad he hadn't given Pavel the option to come and grateful to Diva for staying behind, as well. Not that either of them hadn't already seen horrors, but there was nothing they could do to rectify the situation.

"How could Magda escape and do such a terrible thing?" Theo asked.

He knew she was capable of letting someone die, as she'd proven when she abandoned her own sister. But this? This was beyond cruel, and not the action of a spiteful and jealous woman.

"This wasn't Magda." Tagan walked around the room, his nostrils flaring. "I smell another scent. Pure evil. Zlo was the culprit."

Zlo! Theo could have kicked himself. That was the cold sensation he'd felt when he'd been in the prison earlier. Zlo's mind had touched Theo's own once before. It left a numbness on his brain, a foggy sense of manipulation. Apparently, Zlo had done the same thing again. If only Theo had recognized the feeling earlier, they might have been able to prevent Magda's escape and the death of two soldiers.

Tagan looked at Theo with sympathetic eyes. "Some things cannot be prevented."

Theo took a step back. *How did he know what I was thinking?*

Then he recalled how Magda had told him the Colobari could smell thoughts and emotions. Not only what someone was currently feeling, but emotions they left behind. That had to be how Tagan had determined Zlo was the evil presence.

"There's nothing more we can do here." Sadness and anger etched Zmey's voice. "I'll send someone to bring back my fallen soldiers and give them an honorable send off to the Forest of Souls."

In silence, the three mourners shuffled their way back to the library. Once they exited the prison domain, cool air replaced the stagnant, sweltering heat of the underground cells, and Theo wiped his brow. Except for their feet echoing against the marble floors of the castle, everything was silent. To Theo, the noise sounded like "Doom, doom, doom." As they neared the library, a faint murmuring inside was filled with worry.

All eyes turned toward them as they entered the room. Zmey's voice choked when he informed the others about the tragedy.

Theo voiced his anger. "This makes me even more determined to put a stop to those evil monsters."

"Me, too." Zmey clenched his fists. "Let's go over once more what our plan of action is. We can't afford any mistakes."

"Our main hope lies with securing the assistance of the Ispolini," Kobur the Eagle said. "With their massive strength and height, they are the only ones who can batter the fortress gates and walls, which will allow our forces to rush inside, rather than being picked off one by one from anyone securing the watchtowers."

Zmey paced. "We all know how risky it is to expect the Ispolini to help, since my mother is the reason for their enchantment, but I have high hopes they'll be willing to assist us."

"Have you thought about offering them something for helping?" Pavel asked.

Zmey stopped pacing. "What did you have in mind?"

Pavel removed his glasses and blew on them, clearing non-existent dust. "Well, from what you all have said about the giants, they wanted to be left alone. You're asking a lot of them. Why not make them a promise that once this is over, no one will bother them again."

"How—?" Theo started.

"I know what you're going to say," Pavel interrupted. "How can anyone keep that promise? There's so much magic here, I would think someone could create a force field around all of Kaleto. I mean, look at the Znahar Tree. That has a protective bubble."

Zmey looked toward Kobur the Eagle. "That sounds like an enticing argument. Is that something the Colobari would be able to accomplish?"

The three priests conferred in low voices in what sounded to Theo like the old tongue. Finally, Kobur replied, "We can further explore the possibility, but as yet, we cannot make any promises."

Zmey nodded. "The Ispolini were honorable and had no quarrels with Tangra's priests. It's a proposal you can present to them, with conditions. I think if they understand that we have a better chance of victory with their help, they'll be more likely to join forces with us."

"A win for them," Pavel said, "will be a win for everyone."

"Except Zlo, Lamia, and Magda," Theo added.

Diva had remained silent, standing with Theo and Pavel, while she listened intently to all that was said. Now she raised the question that was on Theo's mind.

"All of that will depend on whether or not you can remove the enchantment on the Ispolini," she said. "According to you, the current conditions—war and the Firebird's untimely rebirth—will enable you to attempt this. But, no one has ever tried the ritual before. What will you do if you can't bring the Ispolini back?"

"Yah," Pavel added. "We need a plan B."

"Our original course of action was to summon the aid of the dragon people to burn down the gates," Kobur started. "But we decided against it because it poses two problems. First, these people are not trained in the art of war. They have lived peacefully in various occupations in villages scattered around Zmeykovo. Second, their power to transform is untested. It has been centuries since they've participated in a war. Since then, the dragon people have intermarried, and their dragon blood runs thin. Even if they can shift into dragons, their powers and abilities are far less then what the royal dragon family can accomplish."

"What about entering the fortress through some of the underground tunnels?" Theo asked.

Kobur shook his head. "We fear that all those will now be well-guarded or blocked. Zlo will not be taken by surprise again. Our current line of defense rests with Zmey's soldiers."

"We brought back a lot of armor and weapons Sitara made," Pavel said. "Will the soldiers be able to set fire to the gates the way you wanted the dragon people to do?"

"Yes," Kobur replied. "They will carry torches ignited with dragon fire."

Dragon fire? Theo mused about that. He hadn't realized that their fire was anything other than ordinary. *I wonder if I can call on my fire when I'm not in dragon form?* He had tried before and failed, but he would ask his dragon spirit when the opportunity arose. Right now, he had to concentrate on his father's battle plans.

Pavel spoke Theo's thoughts. "How does dragon fire work differently than regular fire?"

Kobur turned to the other Colobari. "Rattan, would you like to explain while Tagan and I go over more details with Zmey?"

The hawk Colobar bowed his head, and Kobur, Tagan, and Zmey left to continue their planning.

"Like any fire," Rattan began, "a dragon's can be used to destroy or refine. The difference lies in the intensity of the flame. What a normal fire can consume in an hour, a dragon's can eradicate in mere minutes due to its corrosive properties."

Pavel's eyes went wide. "So, it's possible if we use dragon fire, we could burn down the gates before anyone had much of a chance to react?"

"That is correct," Rattan said, "although, as you know, getting to Kaleto Fortress is an arduous task, and discovery before we arrive is possible."

"Not to mention that they'll be expecting us, as well, and will be on the lookout," Diva added.

"This is true," Rattan replied. "Another aspect of dragon fire that has been observed on occasion throughout the ages is its magical abilities. Few dragons have possessed this power, however." The Colobar glanced at Theo. "Consequently, it's unknown the extent of what those who possess this ability can do."

Magic! Theo's skin prickled with excitement. He wondered if he possessed such powers. Was that why the Colobar had looked at Theo? Did the man know something Theo didn't. Or if not know, suspect or sense something more to Theo's abilities?

He couldn't resist. He had to find out more. "What kind of magic have dragons had?"

Rattan thought for a moment. "The only recorded ability was to accurately manipulate the direction and intensity of flames. However, it's been speculated that dragons have the capacity to breathe more than fire, although none here in Zmeykovo have recorded that in our history."

"What do you mean?" Theo asked. "What else besides fire could a dragon breathe?"

"The elements," Rattan said. "Anything that has to do with earth, air, fire, water, and spirit."

Diva's eyes shone. "Are you saying a dragon can manipulate these, maybe even combining them?"

"That is what some Colobari from the past have believed." Rattan nodded. "Although it has yet to be proven."

If it's true, the possibilities are endless, Theo thought. If he had that ability, or if Diva did, they could hurl boulders simply with their breath. And so much more. His mother had once told him he could control the elements with his sword's magic. If he could combine that with his dragon abilities … Imagining the enormity of that power made his brain hurt. In the wrong hands, that power could prove disastrous.

Zmey and the other two Colobari rejoined the group.

"We have finalized our plan," the dragon king said. "The Colobari will attempt to break the curse on the Ispolini at first light. Rattan's earlier research with the *Lodge of Light and Lodge of Darkness* has uncovered a ritual that requires harnessing Tangra's power, but the priests must perform the ritual when the morning rays strike the rock formations. It is essential the Colobari are protected at all times so they can complete the ritual without interruption. I'll send my Knights of Light to accompany them."

"Should someone go to the site earlier to scout out the area for dangers?" Theo asked. "I remember that those stone structures were close to the fortress. Lamia and Zlo could have their demons keeping watch."

"Excellent point." Zmey nodded. "I will get volunteers—"

"No need. I can go and bring Pavel and Diva along." He cast a glance at them, and they nodded.

"That's settled, then." Zmey resumed his battle updates. "Our other soldiers will be scattered throughout the mountains, to keep an eye on matters. Whether or not we secure the Ispolini's help, my soldiers will be ready to storm the fortress at my command. The Samodivi and Kukeri also have their own strategies in place."

"What about the suffocating water?" Theo asked. "Now that Magda has escaped, she'll attempt to harm everyone with Lord Vodnik's help."

"A soldier has been sent to gather Rusalki underwater belts," Zmey responded. "We'll have them by nightfall."

Theo breathed a sigh of relief. He didn't want anyone else to have to suffer what he had experienced when trapped in the Vodnik's suffocating water. He and Pavel each had their own belt to protect them, but he wasn't certain whether Diva did or not. They would wait to leave until they knew there were enough belts for everyone.

"The only matter remaining is to secure the Golden Apple once we retrieve it," Zmey said. "I suggest we take with us the special box that Kosara created for it. This will tone down the apple's power and prevent a struggle within our own ranks for its possession."

Diva nodded. "I think Theo should be the one to handle this task. He has proven already that he can withstand the apple's pull, and he is well-suited to protecting it once it's in his possession."

"I completely agree," Zmey said as he looked at Theo. "I will go with you shortly to retrieve the box from the Chamber Room."

Theo's heart raced. *Nothing like pressure.* But, even so, he felt confident he wouldn't fail his father. Even though the Golden Apple had messed with his mind when he harvested it, Theo's nature wasn't driven by power or the desire to rule, unlike Lamia or even Magda. He could only imagine how the apple affected their psyches.

"Do you know where Lamia may have put the Golden Apple?" Theo asked. "The last time it was brought to her in the ballroom, where she was going to perform the ritual. If they're expecting us to attack, it's likely she's hidden it somewhere."

"I don't." Zmey turned to Diva. "My daughter, do you recall anything of your time in the fortress? Something that would give us a clue where Lamia might keep the real Golden Apple that Magda brought there, if indeed she really did this time?"

"I'm sorry I brought all this trouble on you." Diva lowered her eyes, and her pale cheeks held a pink hue. Before Theo could tell her that it wasn't her fault, she continued, "When I first was revived, I didn't recall anything that had happened. Now, vague memories are returning. I remember a room filled with clothes. Lamia and Magda were there, laughing. Lamia put the box with the fake Golden Apple into a dresser. After that, my memory fades. Maybe I'll remember where the room is by the time we go look for the apple."

"Thank you." Zmey lifted Diva's face. "Don't punish yourself for what you had no control over. Magda could have enchanted anyone. You just happened to be there and were someone she tried to put the blame on. We'll all get through this. I have no doubt we'll succeed."

"Yah," Pavel wrapped his arm around her waist. "You're so strong. Just think of how much worse it could have been if Magda had tried that on anyone else."

Diva nudged him with her elbow, but she smiled.

"I think we're ready," Zmey said. "Tomorrow, I'll command my soldiers to prepare for the attack."

Chapter 15
Warning from the Sky

THEO STUFFED THE SPECIAL BOX Kosara had given him into his backpack. He wanted to embrace Zmey's optimism that their mission would be successful. Past encounters with the enemy, however, made Theo's stomach churn. He had an uneasy feeling something was going to go terribly wrong.

Success required more planning. Theo added to his backpack his new Rusalki belt and other items he hoped would give them the advantage over their enemies. He had a plan for how to get the apple without being caught, but he hadn't wanted to let anyone else know yet. Too many ears hearing his plans could mean too many mouths revealing something he wanted to keep secret.

He hefted on his backpack, grabbed his sword and bow and arrows, took one look around his room, and left, hoping he'd be able to return. When he passed by the small ballroom that held what he called the dragons-in-love statue, Theo stopped and rubbed his medallion, which had become warm.

The statue spoke to me before. I wonder if it can give me advice again.

He stepped into the room and gazed into the eyes of each dragon, searching for answers.

"Your children are fighting each other," Theo said. "Zmey loves Lamia and wants to save her. I'm sure in her heart she loves her brother, too, but she's under the influence of Zlo."

Theo blinked. *Did the dragons' eyes just flash red?*

Had the loving parents despised Zlo as well? Maybe they had tried to warn Lamia of his deadly influence.

Whatever had happened, the statues remained lifeless, so he continued, "I can't believe Lamia would do all these terrible things by her own free will. I think maybe, you, too, Hala, became possessed of some evil influence. Maybe Zlo enchanted you, too?"

This time, nothing happened when he mentioned that cursed name.

"I'm sure you would have hated all this fighting. It's tearing Zmeykovo and the people apart." Theo paused.

Should I mention the Ispolini?

He shook his head. Probably better not. Since Hala had started that war, it was better not to bring up the subject. He didn't know what other history or bad blood existed between her and the giants.

"Anyway, I was hoping you'd provide us your protection, especially for your children." He stared a long time at the statue, hoping for a sign or some response, but received none. "Please, if there's any way you can help us save Zmeykovo, I'd be grateful."

"Are you ready for the battle?" a voice said from behind him.

Theo jumped and spun around. "As ready as I can be."

"Who were you talking to?" Diva looked around the room. "Is Pavel hiding here?"

"No, I'm right behind you," Pavel said.

Theo shrugged. "I was just wondering if things would be different now if Zmey and Lamia's parents were here."

"We can't change what is. We can only try to make the future better." Diva turned her eyes to the statue. "All those times I've seen this statue and never realized they were my ancestors, my grandparents. It's been such a big surprise."

She reached out and laid a hand on each of the dragons. Almost immediately, she jerked away and rubbed her fingertips as if stung.

"What happened?" Theo and Pavel both asked.

Theo touched the statue, but only felt its coldness.

"I saw something," Diva whispered. "Zmey and Zunitza were dressed in royal outfits and were wearing their crowns. I think Zunitza was going to tell me something, but the vision startled me, and I took my hand away."

"Try again." Theo encouraged her.

She touched the dragons' faces once more. A few moments later, she shook her head and removed her hands. "Nothing this time."

Theo sighed. "Well, I guess we should get going so we can make sure no one's hiding where the Colobari need to perform their ritual." He handed his bow and arrow to Pavel. "I brought these for you to use if you want."

Theo had decided that he couldn't protect his friend all the time. Pavel was good with the weapon. Both Theo and Diva would be there to keep an eye on their friend, but Theo had to let go and allow Pavel to be part of the battle if his friend wanted to.

Pavel's eyes brightened. "Wow! Thank you. I just hope it doesn't change into a snake when I'm using it."

Theo laughed. "I'm sure it won't."

"If it does," Pavel said, "I still have this neat sword Sitara made for me. I can't wait to see what the magic in it does."

"Let's hope you don't have to use it," Theo said. "I guess if we don't get going, we'll never know."

Daylight was fading fast by the time they exited the castle. Throughout the meadow, weapons clashed, feet beat the earth, and soldiers panted as they practiced swordsmanship. Other men inspected weapons and armor, ensuring everything was ready for the upcoming confrontation.

Zmey stood before a group of soldiers and spoke with a steady, commanding voice. "The battle ahead of us will be arduous and dangerous. Lives on both sides are bound to be lost, but we fight for the freedom and peace of Zmeykovo."

Cheers rose and men held their weapons high.

"It's critical to remain focused on the task you all have been assigned," Zmey continued. "Look out for your fellow soldiers, and they will look out for you. We must be disciplined and united as we venture forth on the morrow. Fighting side by side as a team, we will succeed!"

Once more, the men cheered and stomped their feet. Vibrations reached Theo. The soldiers quieted and kept their eyes focused on their king as he spoke and appointed leaders among them. Heads nodded and fists bumped each other as men congratulated one another for their well-deserved assignments.

Will I ever be a leader like that? Theo thought. *Will Zmeykovo's army ever look in such admiration at me as they now do at my father?*

Diva nudged him. *"They will,"* she thought back. *"You may not have noticed it, but I've seen the way people cast glimpses at you when you pass by."*

"And not just the pretty girls," Pavel said out loud, and Theo laughed.

"They hold you in great esteem," Diva added. *"The boy from the human world who is one of them."*

Zmey's soldiers re-checked weapons, tightened armor, and gathered supplies. They fell into formation. With his sword drawn, Zmey stood in front of one group. He gave them a final word of encouragement and sounded the command to move out.

The men kept their eyes fixed on the horizon as they marched down the mountain toward Kaleto Fortress. They would hide in designated locations, so they were ready to attack at Zmey's command in the morning. Other soldiers remained practicing in the meadow. These would travel with their king and the Colobari in the pre-dawn hours to safeguard the priests during their ritual to lift the giants' curse.

Zmey looked Theo's way and at last separated himself from his army. "I see you, too, are ready to leave."

"Yes, Father." Theo nodded. "We have our Rusalki belts, weapons, Kosara's box, and everything else we'll need to scout out the area."

Zmey grasped both Theo's and Diva's shoulders. "Stay safe, my children. And protect your friend. Send word if you encounter any challenges."

"Then they'll need me to accompany them." Boo fluttered down from a tree he must have been keeping watch from. "I'm a good messenger."

Theo bent down and ruffled the magpie's feathers. "You are that, and an even better friend. We're happy to have you join us."

Diva blew a whistle to call Sur, Shar, and Whirl. Theo had decided to fly on his deer companion rather than shift into a dragon. He would save his energy for the battle to come. Sur had told them the rest of the herd would join them before morning light.

As he was about to get on his deer, a high-pitched, out-of-breath voice called out, "My King! My King!"

Theo glanced in the direction of the voice, and at the same time, Zmey turned to look. The true dragon king smiled when Sly approached Theo.

"Sly!" Theo said. "I was wondering what happened to you. I was worried."

The Vodnik hopped around. "Sly worried, too. And scared. So scared."

"What happened Sly?"

"Oh oh oh." The Vodnik covered his face with his webbed paws, as if blotting out some horrendous sight. "I try to stop him."

"Who?"

"Father." Sly shook and scrunched down on the ground.

Sly went up against Lord Vodnik? Theo couldn't imagine the skittish water creature confronting the king of the Vodni. That monster was cruel and had no sympathy for anyone, not even his own people.

Theo crouched beside Sly and whispered, "What did you do? Did he hurt you?"

No welts or bloody gashes plastered Sly's flesh. Theo sighed in relief. Whatever harm Lord Vodnik had done was not physical. Although damage to Sly's fragile emotional state could be just as devastating.

"No, no, no. He never see Sly. I sneak and hide." He removed his hands from his face. "I try to stop Father from leaving swamp."

"So he wouldn't do that terrible thing you couldn't tell us about?" Theo asked.

"Yes, yes. I cause all kinds of trouble at home. Make brothers and sisters fight everywhere. Father so so angry." Sly darted his big buggy eyes around and whispered, "But bad bad witch came. Now Father gone with her."

"Thank you for trying. That was quite brave of you, Sly."

Theo didn't need to trouble Sly with the information that Lord Vodnik's suffocating water would no longer hurt anyone if he and Magda succeeded in creating it from the moisture in the air. He wasn't sure if Sly would understand. The creature was like Pavel. Once either of them got an idea in their heads, it was hard to convince them otherwise.

"Brave?" Sly's eyes popped out even more. "No, Sly failed. Father gone. Now I so so scared. Afraid to go home."

"You know what, Sly?" Theo leaned closer. "We're all leaving. I think Jabalaka will be scared, too. Can a brave fellow like you stay here at the castle and protect him?"

"Master scared?" Sly got up and hopped around. "Oh oh oh. Must protect Master. He Sly's friend." With that, Sly scampered away, likely to the secret passageway in the rose garden that led to the library.

Diva smiled at Theo as he stood and dusted off dirt from his clothing. She nudged him and thought, *"See, you're already acting like a king. Look at how you encouraged Sly."*

FLYING DOWN THE NORTH FACE of Cherna Mountain quickly brought Theo and his friends to the outcropping of grotesquely shaped rocks where the Colobari had advised the group to wait. Theo recalled his first trip here. It had taken hours of foot travel. He didn't miss the aching feet or the dangers he and his traveling companions had encountered along the way. This recent trip to the same location had been pleasant. Not only had the vast landscape been free of the presence of their enemies, but also the panoramic view of Zmeykovo was breathtaking. The setting sun had cast an orange glow over Rusalki Bay, making the water appear to be dancing with fire.

After they landed, Boo said, "I'll take a closer look around." Without waiting for Theo to object, the magpie darted off into the sky.

"Don't worry about him." Diva came to Theo's side. "He'll be fine."

"I guess." Theo nodded. "But I didn't think Boo would go off by himself when there could be dangers."

"He's come a long way from the scared little bird you first knew."

"I know, but I still worry about him." Theo shrugged. "He's so little, and he doesn't have the fighting ability we do."

Pavel shook his head. "Little can be good. It means he can hide quickly and in small places."

"I know, but—"

Diva interrupted. "He's a good scout. My sisters have been thrilled to have him be their messenger and lookout."

"Okay, okay." Theo threw his hands up in the air. "Two against one. I won't worry about Boo."

He had to believe that the magpie could take care of himself. *Boy, it's tough letting go and allowing my friends to demonstrate their strengths.*

Even so, Theo scanned the sky where the magpie had disappeared. If anything happened to the bird, Theo would be devastated, knowing he could have scouted the area by himself, without putting Boo in danger.

The sun soon set, and a rumbling grew in the distance. Sur snorted, giving a sharp wheeze, while Shar flicked his tail. Whirl bounded from side to side, the orb between his horns flashing from one color to another, as if he wasn't certain what was going on.

Pavel went over and rubbed the deer's flank. "Shh, shh. It's just thunder. A storm's coming in." Turning to Theo, Pavel said, "I didn't hear anything about rain in the forecast."

Theo rolled his eyes, and then tuned in his dragon sight and sound toward the direction of the rumbling. "I don't think—"

"They're coming!" Boo flew like a rocket back toward Theo. "Lots and lots of them. Harpies, Navi, and other demons."

That's what Theo had feared. He'd picked up the beating of wings and the screeches and wails of creatures.

"I can see them now." Diva pointed toward a dark cloud that blotted out the stars. It advanced like a swarm of bees.

"I'll get help," Boo screeched.

"No, please hide, my friend!" Theo pleaded with the magpie. "You'll have to fly straight into them. You'll never outfly them."

Boo shook his head, ruffled his feathers, and zipped away, back toward the castle.

The smell of death and rot overpowered Theo as Harpies drew nearer. They filled the sky. There were more than had been sent to attack them any other time.

"How are we going to fight them all?" he thought to his friends.

"One at a time," Pavel responded. *"We have the mountains at our back. We'll pile them up the way we did those nasty green dragons once before."*

Theo shivered at how close they'd come that time. Pavel's untried invention had actually worked. He called it a Pavel-dome, his personal invisible fence. It had created an electrical field around them. Each time one of the small dragons slammed into the barrier, the creature was electrocuted and hurled backward. But every encounter also weakened the electrical field, and the dragons had almost overpowered them. Fortunately, Diva had arrived, chasing away the remaining creatures.

This time, Theo didn't have to rely on Diva alone to save the day. He had reserved his strength in case they found themselves in a situation like this. Now, it was time to shift into a dragon and call on his dragon spirit's power.

Theo no longer had to think to transform. Anger at the approaching hoards ramped up his body heat. His torso expanded, and his limbs thickened and ended in dagger-sharp claws. Fiery-red wings erupted from the scales on his back. All his senses became even more refined. He could hear an enemy approach before one had the chance to catch him unaware. Nodding once to Diva and Pavel, Theo stretched his wings and leapt into the sky.

Keeping the oncoming monsters between him and his friends, Theo exhaled fire. *"How far can we make the flames go?"* he asked his dragon spirit. *"Can we harness the power of the wind?"*

"First, we must stir up the wind," the dragon spirit replied.

Theo thrust his wings with as much strength as he could. Trees bent against the force, their leaves racing around him in the whirlwind. Once more, Theo took a deep breath, held it, and forced out fire toward the approaching enemies.

Flames divided and burst off into a multitude of streams, scorching Harpies, Navi, and other demons Theo hadn't yet encountered. The stench of burnt flesh and feathers filled the air. Creatures in the frontline screeched and veered to the side, but Diva's and Pavel's arrows caught the monsters before any could escape. Harpies and the baby-like Navi tumbled to the ground.

Despite all their efforts, the swarm of demons surged forward.

"How are we going to defeat so many?" Theo asked his dragon spirit.

"I smell help."

And then, Theo did, too. He smelled the scent of fear and death from his enemies.

A whirlwind swept thousands of bats into the midst of the demon hoard. The mammals relentlessly attacked the Harpies and Navi with savagery, tearing at the bird-women's wings and clawing at their eyes. The Navi were the first to retreat, and then the Harpies.

Arrows and spears hurtled through the air and pierced the remaining enemies. The demons turned their forces around, but were now caught in an onslaught from in front and behind. Dozens of demons spiraled to the ground, the unearthly sound of their dying shrieks making Theo cringe. Soon, those remaining alive dispersed.

Everything went quiet. A multitude of Harpies, Navi, and demon corpses cluttered the ground. Blood and gore stained their lifeless wings.

The bats formed a funnel and swirled toward the ground, where they turned into Drakus. From the other side, Theo could now glimpse the Kukeri, Samodivi, and Zmey's soldiers astride the six-winged deer. The riders saluted Theo before returning to the castle or the other places they had been stationed.

Theo let out a long breath. Relieved that Boo had come through. He'd arrived at the castle in time. And, more importantly, the magpie had reached it safely.

Theo returned to the ground and shifted into boy form. "Drakus, thank you for coming. If you hadn't arrived when you did, I don't know …" He dreaded thinking what would have become of him, Diva, and Pavel.

The Oupir bowed. "That's what friends are for. I was in the vicinity, expecting some kind of attack. I can't remain long, since midnight approaches, and I must return to my coffin. I'm glad the hoard didn't wait much longer to make their move."

A tingling sensation raced over Theo. They weren't out of trouble yet. He scanned the sky. There! From the direction of the castle. A black blur sped through the sky. Theo tuned into the creature. It was Boo! The magpie was returning and screaming.

Theo picked out the frantic words: "Lamia's coming!"

Behind Boo, a massive golden creature swooped along the currents. Her wings flapped as if she were in no hurry. In the darkness, her eyes blazed red like two glowing embers. Theo felt no fear coming from her. Only anger as her eyes fixed on him, burning into his soul.

Boo landed and zipped into a crevice. Theo was glad the magpie decided to hide this time. Pavel, too, crouched against the boulders, with Diva standing next to him. Both held arrows nocked in their bows, ready to release them if Lamia came within range of the weapons.

Good, Theo thought. No heroics from his friend this time. *If he stays next to Diva, he'll be fine.*

Lamia let out a deafening roar as she circled overhead. Her tongue flicked in and out like a flame, and white plumes of smoke shot out of her nostrils, but no fire. The thrusts of her wings stirred up gravel into biting weapons, and the gusts uprooted trees. As she circled, she kept her eyes pinned on Theo.

Finally, she spoke to his mind. *"This is the only warning I'll give you. Stay away from the fortress. If you don't, I'll destroy everyone you love. As soon as I can unlock the enchantment of Kosara's golden box, I'll achieve the greatest power ever known to Zmeykovo."*

She circled once more, let out a roar, and flew away. A black crow crept out of a tree branch and followed Lamia.

Theo thought about what Lamia said. Magda must have secured the real Golden Apple in the box the fake one had been in. But something else Lamia had said nagged at him. Why was the box locked this time?

Theo couldn't help thinking, *Who's playing what game?*

Chapter 16
The Great Awakening

JULY 16

THE DAY TO AWAKEN the Ispolini from their centuries-old dream had arrived. In the pre-dawn hour, Theo shifted into a dragon and surveyed the land. All remained quiet. He hadn't expected Lamia or her forces would return, but he didn't want any further surprises when the Colobari arrived.

As he circled his campsite from above, he pondered his dream. The aroma of hay and leaves the night before had lulled him into a deep sleep. His dream hadn't been anything extraordinary. He'd envisioned his human mother going about her daily routines without him there. Nia attended school and laughed with her friends. It brought a tickle to his throat and heaviness to his eyes, but he held back the tears.

He wasn't certain whether the emotion was because he missed his mother and sister or because of his guilt for feeling more at home in Zmeykovo than in Selo. He'd wanted to think about his family, but he'd pushed them to the back of his mind.

In his dream, he'd also seen Zima proud and haughty, but with a great love for his land. Others Theo hadn't known rushed past him like a waterfall. All those who had lost their lives since Lamia began her rampage thirteen years ago called out to him from their orbs in the Forest of Souls. Most of all, he had felt Zunitza's presence in his dream. Her love for him overpowered his senses.

The problems facing Zmeykovo were more serious than whatever might be going on in Selo.

Or were they?

Am I deceiving myself? Am I pretending that Selo is safe and my family is fine because Zmeykovo is more of a home to me now?

Was this the price of growing up? Leaving behind all that he knew and loved and making his own way in the world … whatever world that might be?

In Selo, he was just a boy trying to be the man of the family. He had no greater purpose. Not that protecting his mother and sister wasn't a noble cause. But here … in Zmeykovo … he could do so much more.

Theo sighed. *This is where I know I belong.*

He pushed aside the thoughts once more. His undivided concentration was needed today so they could defeat Zlo and Lamia. He couldn't let his mind wander to other matters. Tomorrow was another day. He could focus on his human family then. The morning was wiser than the evening as his grandmother always said.

In the distance, torches lit the sky. A group of soldiers approached. Three groups, in fact. Theo tuned in his dragon senses. It was the Colobari, arriving from three different directions. Theo did one more turn around the rock formations, but detected no threats. All that remained of yesterday's attack was a pile of ashes. Theo had burned the dead demons to a crisp.

He swooped back to where Pavel and Diva were taking down the tents. Boo had left earlier to inform Zmey about Lamia's arrival the night before and her warning. Theo wanted to ask his father about her claim that the box containing the Golden Apple was enchanted.

"The Colobari are on their way," he said after he shifted back into a boy.

"Everything's a-okay?" Pavel asked. "No more Lamia or Harpies?"

Theo shook his head. "No, I doubt we'll see her again until we battle her at the fortress."

A sudden chill spread over Theo, starting on the inside and making its way out. He rummaged in his backpack for a jacket and put it on. The air was cool, but Theo couldn't help believe the feeling came more from his fear of what was to come.

The three of them remained in silence, moving about their tasks like shadows. Theo could sense both Diva and Pavel felt their own anxieties.

Kobur the Eagle arrived first, from the group that traveled down the mountain from the direction of the castle. Among them was Zmey. Theo's heart felt joy and pride. His father's presence brought Theo a sense of security. He could let go of his responsibilities for the moment and let his father be in control.

Zmey approached and said, "Well done, son. I hear you fought bravely and have developed new abilities."

"Yes, but Lamia said—"

Kobur cleared his throat. "We have no time to waste. The sun will rise soon. We must move to higher ground right away. Talk of battle can come later."

Tagan the Falcon and Rattan the Hawk arrived with their soldier guards. They surrounded Zmey and Kobur, further preventing Theo from speaking with his father. The troops marched out, following Kobur over the mountainous terrain to a plateau, nestled at the foot of the peaks and overlooking the stone structures that jutted up from the land below.

From this height, one of the stone structures clearly stood out, rising above the others. The monstrous figure possessed what looked like three heads. Around the area where the mouths would be found were jagged rocks resembling frightening teeth set within a snarling face. Massive boulders were fused together to form limbs a body-builder would envy.

The Colobari positioned themselves at the edge of the plateau, facing this enchanted giant. The soldiers spread out around the edges. Zmey, Theo, Diva, and Pavel huddled near each other in the middle.

The north wind was fierce and chilly as it swooped down the mountainside, making the priests' white robes billow like sails during a tempest. The men, however, remained standing upright. Their eyes closed and their faces solemn, the priests held aloft their sacred staffs, each a hair's breadth from touching the others.

Low at first, the chants grew in intensity, forming words. Theo tried to grasp their meaning, but he forgot each utterance as soon as the priests spoke it. All he could recall was the harmony of the song that echoed throughout the mountains.

Is it magic or mind control? It was just like in the book, *Lodge of Light and Lodge of Darkness.* Theo hadn't been able to understand the sacred rituals written there, no matter how hard he had tried.

With slow, measured steps, the priests, in a trancelike state, moved in a circular motion from right to left. In the *Lodge* book, Theo had discovered that the ancient Thracians thought of this direction as moving from a lower, earthly level of consciousness to a higher, sacred, celestial one, which filled the participants with healing power.

And now the Colobari would heal the Ispolini.

As the men moved, a soft, white glow emanated from their staffs. The surrounding darkness made the action all the more mysterious. A faint humming seemed to come from the Celestial Turtles at the tips of the staffs. The sound mingled with the priests' murmured words until Theo couldn't distinguish one from the other. The air shimmered and glowed, and the ground vibrated with energy.

Theo stood mesmerized as the Colobari continued in this manner, their steps never faltering, their arms remaining steady.

A rosy hue soon lightened the sky. Even with their eyes closed, the priests must have sensed the change. Their pace quickened, and their voices became louder. Still, the words evaded Theo moments after they were spoken.

As the sun rose from the direction of Rusalki Bay, golden rays struck the Colobari's staffs. Perfectly timed with that, the men touched the staffs together. A beam of light shot off the tip of each turtle's head. Gold, silver, and bronze, like the staff themselves. The lights twisted together like a serpent and formed a glowing star with seven rays. Each light shone brighter than the last. The star spun faster and faster, bending into the shape of an ouroboros, the symbol of infinity and rebirth.

Shouting as one, the Colobari hurled the light toward the tall rocky structure.

Light shattered the darkness.

A deep, eerie silence reigned.

No one dared to breathe.

Then he heard it. A faint rumbling. Followed by a slight shifting of the ground as if it were alive and waking from slumber. Scattering pebbles turned into tumbling rocks. The earth heaved, and Theo grabbed onto Pavel and Diva. Zmey wrapped his arms around all of them while soldiers around the perimeter moved in closer.

The rumbling grew into a roar. Boulders split apart, and an avalanche of debris poured down the mountainside. Huge chunks of rock fragments pinged off of the plateau. Everyone moved nearer to the Colobari, where a bubble of calm lay within the surrounding chaos.

Even though he expected it, Theo's heart raced as the tallest rocky structure crumbled. From within, an enormous hairy being emerged. He towered above them, even as they stood on the plateau. The Ispolin had three heads with a single eye in each. These eyes glowed, outshining the light from the twisting ouroboros that continued to travel down his torso. Stretching his bulging muscles and rotating his shoulders, the giant shook off the remaining rocks. The cracking boomed like thunder as they hit the ground.

The giant stepped out of the rubble that had encased him for centuries. He scanned the area, stopping when he faced the direction of the Colobari. In two strides, the giant was at the plateau. His eyes flashed red with a menacing glare. A grin spread across each face, and he opened his mouths wide, exposing teeth like spikes that even Lamia should fear.

Theo covered his ears as an earth-shattering roar shook the mountainside.

Then the awoken Ispolin did something Theo would have never expected if he hadn't seen it happening right in front of him. The giant bent on one knee before the Colobari. His heads became level with those of the priests.

"He's going to eat them!" Pavel screamed.

"He is not." Zmey grabbed hold of Pavel as he tried to rush forward. "The Ispolini have quarrels only with dragons. No one else is their natural enemy."

Pavel squirmed in Zmey's grasp. "Then he's going to eat you. And Theo. And Diva!"

"No, he won't." Diva spoke so softly that Theo almost missed her words. Her eyes had lit up, and she focused her attention on the monstrous-sized being only feet in front of them. "He's … magnificent."

She had been sad that she'd never lived during the time of the Ispolini. Now, she had the chance to meet at least one giant.

The awoken Ispolin swiveled one head Diva's way. His brow narrowed, then shot up in a questioning look. His eye seemed to be analyzing her, trying to understand what she was. Next, he looked at Theo. Again, a puzzled look crossed his face. His mouth formed a grin when he cast a glance at Pavel, who squirmed and turned pale under the scrutiny. Zmey was the only one who brought forth a growl from the giant.

Rattan the Hawk raised his hand to the Ispolin, and the giant turned his attention back to whatever silent conversation he was having with the Colobari. They remained that way, as still as statues while the sun inched its way up the sky.

At length, the giant stood and lowered his heads to the priests. They returned the gesture.

Kobur approached Zmey. "The Ispolin king has agreed to the terms we have set forth. His people will assist in demolishing the fortress walls, but he will not force any of them to participate in the battle."

"They?" Theo glanced around. Only one stone structure had transformed, the king. The first light of dawn had already come and gone. "Can you still bring the rest of the giants back?"

"Yes, Young Dragon Prince. We have not completed our task." Kobur turned back to Zmey. "The Ispolin king understands we may not be able to create a barrier of such great magnitude around them, but he will accept whatever protection and isolation we can provide his people."

"Tell him we all appreciate their help," Zmey said. "I am not my mother. What she did was horrendous. The Golden Apple's power changed her. We have many precautions now to try to prevent that."

The Ispolin king growled. "And yet, the apple poses a threat even now. We are in the same situation we were in when Hala reigned. When we roamed the land, Hala's daughter was easily corrupted. How can we be certain future generations will not succumb to the lust for power?"

"Because this is the future of our land." Zmey gestured toward Theo and Diva.

Once more, the Ispolin king stared. Not with anger or hatred, but with curiosity. He tilted all three heads slightly.

"Perhaps it will be a better world," the giant replied, giving Theo and Diva another long stare before turning away and nodding to Kobur. "My people are restless. I can feel them struggling to be free. Let us proceed."

Theo, too, could feel the stones beneath his feet quivering. Tension filled the air. Fear. Joy. Anger. Many emotions vibrated around him. He didn't fear the reprisal of the Ispolini when they returned. Without a doubt, the giant king could control his people.

Kobur, Tagan, and Rattan strode to the edge of the plateau. Once more, they raised their staffs and formed a pyramid with the tips. When the ouroboros light shot out of the mouths of the Celestial Turtles, this time the priests sent it downward. The plateau shook, and a loud cracking resounded from all directions. A deep abyss split open. All along its length, the light branched out like lightning. The earth groaned. It heaved and glowed with its burden. For as far as Theo could see, slivers of light sped across the entire land.

The rock structures by the mountain exploded, hurling debris in all directions. Each Ispolin who emerged bellowed. Their voices pounded the air with a deafening clamor. Some giants sported three heads, while others only one, but the single eye of each Ispolin glowed red.

Their king raised his arms, and the giants quieted. To Zmey, the revived king said, "My people will join us here from everywhere they have been imprisoned."

Tremors from their stomping feet shook the earth. In the distance, trees swayed, and birds, disturbed from their morning activities, took flight.

It would have been impossible for Zmey's enemies waiting in Kaleto Fortress not to have witnessed the awakening of the giants.

Chapter 17
The Sacrifice

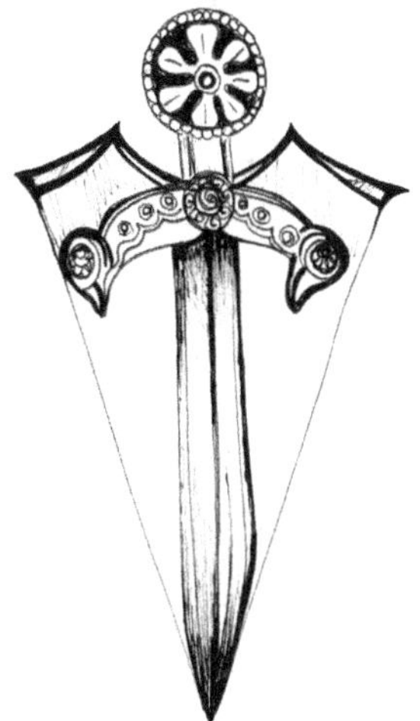

FLOCKS OF FLYING CREATURES gathered over all parts of Zmeykovo, blotting out the sun. They flew en masse toward the plateau.

"The Harpies are coming back!" Pavel shouted.

Theo tuned in his dragon senses to the approaching hoards. "They're not Harpies. They're … eagles."

This was his dream made reality. After Magda had poisoned him, Theo had had a dream—or perhaps a vision—about both eagles and the Ispolini. He hadn't known then what it meant.

"They're coming to help us in the battle," Diva said. "They're the messengers of the gods."

"Did you call them?" Pavel asked.

Diva's special gift, granted to her on her thirteenth birthday, was the ability to summon birds for assistance.

She shook her head. "No, I think they've come because the Ispolini have awoken. I've read stories about how eagles have aided Zmeykovo in the past."

Soon, the area surrounding the plateau filled with the beautiful birds. Some perched on stone structures, while others continued to soar overhead. The echo of their screeches pounded in Theo's brain, so he toned down his dragon hearing. He wanted to enjoy the sight and sound of the newest army to join the cause.

Ispolini, too, filled the mountainside. Their shouts and chatter boomed like music from an earsplitting rock concert. Men and women both remained to fight for the return of their land. Their reasons may have varied. Some wanted peace. Others were eager to fight. Both restless and weary from their long sleep, they desired to return to the way of life they had experienced before.

The Colobari held their staffs high in the air. Once more, the metal glowed. The screeching and shouting ceased.

Zmey raised his sword. "Let us go forth, united, to rid the land of the curse of those consumed with power."

Feet stomped and voices shouted, "Urrah!"

"My sister and her master have wrought their destruction on our beautiful home too long," Zmey continued. "We once lived here in peace with one another, despite our differences. Let us do so again."

Theo was glad his father didn't mention Hala. Although the thought was likely forefront in the minds of the giants, to name that evil one would likely have filled the Ispolini with anger—and one directed at Zmey, rather than at Lamia and Zlo. It was better to concentrate on the menace at hand and not bring back painful memories. After all, the past could not be undone, but the future could be made better.

"We march now to Kaleto Fortress!" Zmey's words resounded amid the stamping of feet and beating of weapons.

Zmey twirled his sword in the air and let out a mighty roar. The Colobari thumped their staffs against the plateau.

The final battle was about to begin.

The giants thundered off like a stampede toward the fortress. Their footsteps shook the earth again. Anger raged in their eyes, but not fear. The site had once been their place of safety. Its destruction was necessary. When they rid Zmeykovo of the menace, they could rebuild. But safety trumped comfort in times of war.

Zmey's soldiers followed. Samodivi and Kukeri were in place as well. Overhead, the newest battalion of eagles soared, keeping pace with the army below. Sur's herd joined them from wherever they had been waiting during the night. The fireballs between their antlers glowed black, a color Theo had never seen before. Flames licked about with a raging intensity. The deer were beyond angry. Desire for the death of those who had wreaked havoc on their homeland consumed the deer.

Before Zmey set out, he grasped Theo and Diva by the shoulders. "The army will keep the enemy occupied so you can locate the Golden Apple. Be safe, my children. And I know you will protect your friend."

"We will, Father," they both said.

Theo spoke the final word with confidence. He'd grown used to the idea that the king of Zmeykovo was his sire. Diva, however, hesitated and spoke it more softly. Although she was confident in so many ways, Theo felt her awe at her family standing. To her, Zmey, whom she'd known about all her life, had always been the ruler of her homeland. To claim kinship was unsettling, but welcome. Theo squeezed her hand, and she smiled.

Zmey gave them one last longing look before he shifted into his majestic white dragon form and flew to the head of the marching army.

Next to Theo, Pavel pouted. "I don't need to be protected."

Theo laughed. "Of course you don't. But you know how parents worry about everyone."

Smiling at Pavel, Diva said, "I need you to keep an eye on Theo. You know how he always stumbles into trouble."

"I can do that." Pavel slid on his backpack and picked up Theo's black bow and arrows. "Do we know how we'll find the Golden Apple? Have you remembered any more, Diva?"

"I think I can find my way once we get inside."

"Good." Pavel nodded. "It's going to be kinda tricky getting through all that fighting. Did either of you think of something to get us into the fortress without being stabbed? I haven't had the time or materials to create any new inventions to do that."

"One sec." Theo retrieved his backpack and pulled out a white scarf. "Remember this?"

Pavel opened his eyes wide. "Your invisibility scarf! I forgot about it. That'll work."

"Great plan," Diva added. "We should get going now. I'll call the deer."

She removed a pin-shaped whistle from her pouch and blew. It made a sound only the animals could hear. A moment later, their companions appeared, and Theo, Pavel, and Diva climbed on and flew to catch up with the armies approaching Kaleto Fortress.

"This is it," Theo thought to Shar. *"Today, we either win the war or lose. I'm going to do whatever I can to make sure we're the victors."*

"I have faith in all of you," Shar responded. *"Keep believing in yourself and what you can do, and you'll be successful."*

Ahead of them, Zmey arrived first at the fortress gates. He let out an earth-shattering roar. From every direction, the dragon king's soldiers poured out of crevices they had been hiding within and surrounded the stronghold, guarding the gates so that no one could escape.

More movement stirred within the forests, waterways, and rocky outcrops. Beings of all kinds crept forward. Some had human forms. Those carried an assortment of weapons. Spears, pitchforks, rocks, sharp-tipped branches. Anything, apparently, they could get their hands onto.

Next came wild beasts, predominated by wolves and bears. Driving them forward was Lesnik, who blew a horn. The forest guardian towered above the trees and looked much like one himself. He raised a hand in salute to Theo, who waved back. Other creatures swarmed out of the trees. Some were more animal than human, having horns, tusks, and hooves.

Webbed, finned creatures surfaced from rivers, streams, and waterfalls. Theo blinked and rubbed his eyes. Vodni were among the throng.

"Do you think Lord Vodnik will punish them?" Theo was glad he'd asked Sly to remain with Jabalaka. The Vodnik had suffered so much already, so often the brunt of his father's wrath. It was likely the others had as well, at least those who had been conquered and lost their true father.

"I think you should not worry about things beyond your control," Shar replied. *"When this is over, Zmey will find ways to ensure the safety of those who have aided their king."*

Theo sighed. His deer companion was right. It was important right now to focus on defeating Lamia and Zlo and retrieving the Golden Apple.

Once more, Theo scanned the area. So many subjects had come to aid their king, but no Rusalki. Vodna kept a tight rein on her kingdom, only assisting when it didn't outright align her with either side. At least they had supplied the needed belts to protect against the suffocating water.

The Ispolini had now reached the fortress. They, too, let out roars as they smashed gates, walls, and towers, demolishing the enemy's defenses with ease. Zmey swooped to the ground and shifted into human form. Behind him, his forces scrambled over the rubble. The attacking army was met by a courtyard filled with the Knights of Darkness, Youdi, and all manner of demons. Radan led the horde, with Bor Stobor by his side. Harpies, Navi, and other winged monsters took to the air and attacked the eagles and deer.

Youda Stana remained noticeably absent. It didn't surprise Theo that the leader of the Youdi would send her people into battle, but remain somewhere safe herself. In that way, she was like Zlo. Sending others to fight their battles and not caring about the individuals who lost their lives. They treated the people they were supposed to protect like pawns, easily disposed of and not worthy of a moment's thought about the lives they led. They were so unlike Zmey who put his people first and led his army.

Noises came from all sides. The battle had begun.

In the air, yellow blood spurted from Harpies. Despite the pain the attackers must have felt from coming in contact with the poisoned blood of the half-bird, half-women creatures, eagles and deer pursued their prey with a frenzy. An eagle seized one monster and ripped it to shreds. Nearby, a deer kicked another Harpy and struck it with antlers.

Theo wanted to weep as other eagles and deer fell victim to counterattacks. He yelled, "No!" as a group of Harpies descended upon a deer and mangled its wings. The animal screeched as it plummeted to the ground, no longer able to fly.

"We have to help him!" Theo shouted to Shar.

Sadness etched Shar's voice as he thought back, "*I cannot. Zmey has commanded Sur, Whirl, and me to keep you to your task. Nothing except immediate danger to you, Diva, or Pavel can deter us from getting you to the fortress.*"

"*But, the herd?*"

"*It is the price of war,*" Shar replied. "*They all knew that losses could be great. Not one of the herd chose to refrain from fighting.*"

Theo turned away. He couldn't bear to see more deer lose their lives.

On the ground, the Ispolini snatched up boulders from the destroyed walls and hurled them into the midst of their enemies with deadly accuracy. Other giants simply swung their massive fists against any creature that dared to venture too close. Blood sprayed, and death followed swiftly for some. Others screamed in agony as their lives were cut short.

Everywhere Theo looked was in a state of turmoil. He couldn't stop any of it if he stayed in the air.

"*It's time for us to land,*" Theo thought to Diva and Pavel. "*Do either of you see a good place for us to get into the fortress?*"

Theo itched to fight and not sneak inside, away from the battle, but he wouldn't disobey his father. Someone had to try to retrieve the Golden Apple. At least this way, Theo thought that Diva and Pavel would be somewhat safe, away from the main conflict. Theo had no doubt that dangers awaited him inside. Zlo, Lamia, and Magda were not present below.

"I suggest we creep along the walls by the mountain," Pavel thought back. *"We'll be out of the direct fighting and also have the protection of Zmey's people who are making sure no one escapes."*

"Let's do it." Theo didn't have to direct Shar, and soon deer and riders found a place to land.

"We're off to fight," Shar thought to Theo. *"We can return in a moment when you've achieved your task."*

"Be safe." Theo sighed and wrapped his arms around his deer companion. *"I wish I could go with you."*

"Don't be so quick to desire death," Shar responded. *"None of us is certain to return from this battle. If Sur, Whirl, or I fail, others will be here to bring you to safety."*

"And now I'll tell you that you *won't fail."* Theo squeezed his companion and friend harder. *"Come back for me."*

Shar snorted and flew away with Sur and Whirl.

Theo wiped away moisture from his eyes. Pavel had wet spots on his sleeves where he'd likely done the same after having a similar conversation with Whirl. Diva's eyes were dry, but filled with pain. More than pain. Anger.

"Yes, I'm angry," she thought to him. *"What a waste of life. All for power and greed."*

"We'll stop them." He reached out to her as he spoke aloud. "This madness has to end."

"It will," Pavel said. "It's time to activate our superhuman power and become invisible."

As Theo took off his backpack and reached inside for the scarf, a massive shadow darkened the sky. Every nerve in his body quivered as his dragon spirit raged to be set free. Lamia had discovered them already. It had to be her.

He tossed the scarf to Pavel, hoping he would use it to hide. Theo drew his sword as he spun around. Behind him, Diva whispered, "Let me go." Taking a chance, Theo peeked over his shoulder. Neither Pavel nor Diva was visible.

"*Please stay hidden*," Theo thought to them. "*You can help me better if you catch Lamia unaware*."

"Fine," Diva grumbled, while Pavel said, "Told ya."

"*I've been waiting for you*," Lamia thought to Theo. "*I knew you were here. I could smell your fear for the safety of your friends*."

Where did she come from? Theo looked up to where his aunt hovered by the mountainside. He scanned for more adversaries, but found none. Beyond her, he discovered what he was looking for. A cave so high up he wouldn't have thought to look there for anyone.

"*It's a shame you're alone*," Lamia continued. "*I so wanted to tear your friend and sister to pieces in front of your eyes before I consumed them. I warned you to stay away*."

Theo didn't take the bait. He wasn't going to get caught up in Lamia's taunts. All he needed was a little more time. "*Dragon spirit, time to power up. Let's see what the two of us and the sword's power can do. We'll strike right between her eyes, I think*."

He hoped that the sword's new powers were able to injure Lamia the way they had Zlo. When he'd first attacked his aunt with the weapon, he'd discovered it had no effect. She had told him the sword couldn't hurt her because she was a blood relative.

Theo called upon the power of the wind. It picked up, howling among the trees. Rocks clattered against the ground as they swirled around like tumbleweeds. He next commanded the wind into the sword. It began to glow white.

"*I don't think so*," Lamia shrieked.

Her eyes blazed with a fury that could burn down the world as she lunged toward Theo.

"I call upon—" Theo began as he touched the Firebird symbol on his weapon.

"No!" Diva and Pavel screamed at the same time.

Theo couldn't stop to look. He had to do this. He would destroy Lamia this time. The power within the sword pulsed, ready to be released. Whatever was coming toward him would have to wait. Even if Theo died fighting Lamia, at least he would put an end to her at the same time.

"—the power of the Fire—"

The world came to a screeching halt. At least for Theo. He stood paralyzed unable to prevent a catastrophe.

Zmey leapt in front of Theo, shoving him to the ground.

The light from the sword went dim as Theo lost his grip.

Lamia's sharp claws ripped through Zmey's chest and down to his waist.

The dragon king's severed ouroboros belt somersaulted through the air.

Zmey fell to the ground, clutching a gaping wound over his punctured heart.

Chapter 18
A Change of Heart

TIME SPED UP. Theo found himself cradling his father's body. Diva had shed the scarf and kneeled by Zmey's other side. The dragon king's eyes were wide with shock. His gushing blood seeped into the ground, drenching their clothing. Despite Theo's pressure on the worst of the ragged wound, the flow refused to cease.

"Why did you do it?" Theo barely choked out the words. "I could have defeated her. Didn't you trust me?"

"I did. I do." Zmey gasped, trying to draw in breath. Each word he spoke came out shallow, broken, weak. "I panicked. You were alone. I couldn't lose you."

"But now I'm going to lose you." Theo sobbed, resting his forehead on his father's hair.

By saving Pavel and Diva, Theo had condemned his father to death. The dragon king wouldn't have been so rash if he'd known Diva was there to watch Theo's back. Too many times, one person had been sacrificed to save another.

Zmey coughed up blood. "Take … care … of … each … other. Don't … be … like …"

The garbled words tore at Theo's heart. "Yes, Father. Diva and I will always be there for each other. We won't be like Lamia."

Diva nodded.

Theo took a moment to look at his sister. So much pain was etched into every inch of her face. Dark circles had formed under her eyes. The skin around them was bunched. Her lips were pinched. And her pale skin had become translucent the way it had when she herself had been on the verge of death.

The only other time Theo had seen a semblance of her grieving was when she'd told him that a Harpy had killed one of her sisters. Neva. That was her name. Diva had been strong then, pushing her grief deep inside her. Now, though, she allowed the tears to flow.

Theo had experienced the same overwhelming grief when he'd thought he'd lost her, so soon after discovering she was his sister. Now, Diva was in the same situation. She had only just known Zmey as her father, and Lamia had taken him away from her.

Zmey uttered more fragmented words, indiscernible to the human ear. Theo caught them with his dragon hearing. "Coming, Zunitza."

The dragon king's heartbeat became weaker and irregular. The flow of blood slowed. Zmey's life was fading, and Theo could do nothing to stop it. This injury was too great for even the ouroboros belt to heal.

With one final faint *thump*, Zmey's heart stopped, and he breathed his last.

Theo closed his eyes and vowed to himself, *Diva and I will stop Lamia. Stop Zlo. We'll take our rightful place as rulers of Zmeykovo and lead the battle.*

The Golden Apple could wait. Theo had to show the troops they could still win. A leader stood among them. Two leaders.

Theo forced the pain away. He couldn't let grief overwhelm him. His thoughts had to be clear. That's when it hit him, and he jumped up.

Why didn't Lamia attack Diva and me when we were so vulnerable?

Theo scanned the area. Pavel remained invisible, and Theo sighed in relief.

What could Pavel do to stop a dragon when the king of Zmeykovo himself fell to her power?

"Well, I could keep an eye on her for one thing," Pavel whispered from behind Theo.

Theo jumped and spun around but couldn't see his friend.

"Gotcha. Payback for when you did that to me." Pavel laughed, but the sound held no joy. "To answer your question, I still have your bow and arrow. Maybe I couldn't kill her, but I could have annoyed the heck out of her if she'd decided to attack you."

"Well, keep the scarf on for now," Theo murmured.

"Yah, yah, I know," Pavel grumbled. "You can't concentrate if you're worried about me. Don't concern yourself. I'll be fine."

Theo elbowed the place where the voice came from and was rewarded with a grunt. He continued his scan of the area and finally caught a glimpse of Lamia in her snake-woman form leaning against the fortress wall. Both parts of the ouroboros belt were joined and encircled her waist once more.

When she saw Theo looking, she clapped and slithered his way. "Bravo. Such a touching sight."

"You beast!" Theo tramped toward her. "You killed my father, your own brother!"

"Technically, he's not quite dead yet." Lamia smirked.

"What? I heard—"

"His heart stop?" She caressed the belt. "Yes, his body has ceased functioning, but his spirit lingers a little longer. He won't be completely gone until—"

She stopped speaking.

Specs of silver dust sparkled in the air.

"—about now," Lamia finished her thought.

Horrified, because he'd witnessed that before when he'd killed Lamia the first time, Theo swiveled around to check on what was happening to Zmey's body.

The end of the dragon king's magnificent existence had begun. His body crumbled into silver dust, swirling above where Zmey had lain. Why was his human body dissolving? Only Lamia's three dragon heads had disintegrated. After that, she'd changed back into human form. And that remained intact. Then he remembered that her spirit had lingered and gone into him. That was why Zlo had been able to revive her.

Diva rose and in seconds had an arrow nocked and pointed in Lamia's direction. Gone was the grief from his sister's face. Anger replaced it.

Theo swung around toward Lamia. "Why didn't you kill us all? Get rid of your entire family? You had the perfect opportunity."

Lamia laughed. "What fun would that have been? As it was, I could relish your pain instead."

"You're a monster." His sword lay between him and Lamia. It would be easy to grab it and put her out of his misery.

"Theo, wait. Look," Diva said.

Where Zmey's blood had soaked into the ground, thorny vines emerged and trailed toward Lamia. She backed away until her body pressed against the fortress.

"Make it go away!" she screamed. Terror filled her eyes.

Has Lamia seen something like this before?

Theo couldn't understand why the vines terrified his aunt. Sure, it was odd, but he'd experienced flowers sprouting from the ground before like this when he was searching for Lamia's hidden souls. When the petals had unfolded, they'd held a clue.

Does Lamia fear this vine will give her a clue or some prophecy about her future?

The thorny vine inched its way forward. When it reached Lamia, it began wrapping around her tail.

"Get it off of me!" she screamed. "I'll do anything you want."

Pavel reappeared and tucked the scarf into the side of his pants. "Why don't you do it yourself? Why would any of us help you after all the evil things you've done?"

Around and around the vine went, enclosing Lamia in a net. When it had her lower body completely surrounded, roses bloomed along the vines. Not any roses. Golden ones just like those Magda had said Zunitza planted near the castle.

Lamia trembled. "No, no. Make her stop!"

"Her? Who?" Theo demanded. Had Lamia lost her mind?

"Your mother. Zunitza. Make her stop!"

A terrible thought crossed Theo's mind. "Did you kill my mother, too? Did the roses by the terrace grow from her blood?"

"Yes and yes! I didn't have a choice."

"Everyone has a choice."

"I'm sorry." Lamia sobbed. "I was selfish, greedy, power hungry. Zlo said he would avenge me. Make them all pay for the death of the man I loved."

Before Theo could respond, the silver dust swarmed around the roses, covering Lamia completely. Lamia's screams and cries for help became muted.

Theo didn't know what to do. He stepped forward, then stopped. It was obvious his parents were serving justice on Lamia. Was that something he should even try to prevent? His parents weren't spiteful. Even after everything Lamia had done, Zmey had wanted to save his sister. Did he think that causing her death would achieve that?

Diva wrapped her arms around Theo's waist. "Whatever is happening is for the best. There's nothing you can do."

Lamia's struggling and cries ceased. The silver dust faded, and the vines untangled from their prey. A beautiful golden rose bush spread out amid the ruins of the day. A sign of hope in the chaotic times. But another wondrous sight lay before them.

Theo rubbed his eyes. "This can't be real."

But it was. Before him Lamia appeared the way she had after he'd slain her: beautiful, youthful, and with legs instead of her snake tail. The one difference was that this time Lamia was alive!

His aunt stood paralyzed. She blinked repeatedly before she let out a gasp and dropped to the ground. "It's over. I'm free. Zlo has no control over me."

"What kind of trickery is this?" Pavel scooted between his friends. "Don't trust her. It's another one of her games."

Theo sent out his dragon senses. The aura of evil surrounding his aunt was no longer evident. He looked at Diva, and she nodded.

"I think this time it's for real." He approached Lamia and held out his hand.

She stood on wobbly legs. Theo couldn't help wonder how long ago she'd lost them to be replaced by her snake tail. Even her pointed ears now had a human appearance. She could tell them her story after they overcame their final threat—Zlo. Theo and Diva could deal with all other traitors after that.

"If you've truly changed and are sorry," Theo said, "help us defeat Zlo."

A sad smile formed on Lamia's face. "That's all I ever wanted from you. I tried—"

Theo held his hand up to stop her. "You still had other motives even then. When this is over, you have crimes to pay for."

Lamia bowed her head. "I understand."

"How can we defeat Zlo?"

"He fears the power of Tangra's light," Lamia replied.

"Then he is finished."

Theo knew what he had to do. It could cost him his life, but perhaps that had been his ultimate fate as the Unborn Hero. He took one more look at Diva. She would make a wonderful ruler. She understood everything about Zmeykovo, and her people loved her. She would make this a better, safer place.

"It's time." He retrieved his sword and raised it high.

Pavel donned the helmet Sitara had given him and withdrew the short sword. The runes glowed with the magic crackling in the air. "Wow! That's awesome and creepy at the same time."

"Let's join the fight." Theo's heart raced as he rushed toward the battle.

A chill swept over him, and the pressure of Zlo's darkness bore down on Theo. The coward lurked nearby, hidden. Theo couldn't think about the monster in any other way. Zlo let his minions slaughter and be slaughtered until he felt he had the upper hand. He wasn't able to achieve power over Zmeykovo and the world on his own. Instead, he had to use Lamia as his puppet. There had to be a way to draw Zlo out before too many more people were killed.

"Where's your master, former master, hiding?" Theo asked.

Lamia looked up and shivered. "I can't feel him anymore. He could be anywhere. With so much smoke, it's difficult to tell."

Theo didn't know where to begin looking. He wanted to join the fight, but he had to be ready when Zlo made an appearance. As he observed everything going on, he appreciated the strength and willpower of Zmey's army. They didn't need Theo's help.

Youdi were being overpowered by soldiers. The weapons of the wicked witches held no power. Sitara had seen to that when he'd laced the runes with silver to make them ineffective. Instead, he'd applied the runic symbols to the weapons Zmey's army wielded. Wind, fire, bolts of lightning, fierce streams of water all shot out of the swords to batter the Youdi. The soldier's shields reflected back to the Youdi any magic they manifested.

The Ispolini had left. Their task to demolish the walls was done. But the Kukeri brothers pummeled anyone who got too close to their fists or clubs. Jega's fire spurted out on the other side of the courtyard, so Theo was glad his friend still lived. Sitara's booming voice told Theo his other fighting friend did as well.

Flying demons shrieked as they fell to the ground after being torn to shreds by the deer and eagles. Navi and other demons were gobbled up by Lesnik. A colony of bats swarming around one victim after another indicated that Drakus had arrived. And arrows flying through the air, followed by death screams, let Theo know the Samodivi had found their marks.

He searched until he found Magda. She flailed her arms at Lord Vodnik, who stood by her side on a tower that had somehow survived the Ispolini, likely due to his aunt's dark magic. Theo tuned in his dragon hearing to find out what was going on. As he suspected, Magda was angry that Lord Vodnik's suffocating water wasn't killing her enemies. The Rusalki belts were keeping the soldiers safe.

The water creature shrugged and said, "Your magic seems to have failed you."

"It's not me," she screeched. "You're incompetent."

Lord Vodnik must have felt Theo's stare. He looked that way and … Theo couldn't believe it. The creature *winked*. Had he actually called the suffocating water?

Lord Vodnik nodded. He squeezed his eyes tight and sent a jumble of messages to Theo. "*One doesn't say no to a witch. Even a greater witch than Magda has those she cannot deny. No one wants Zlo to rule Zmeykovo.*"

Theo took a step back. How did the creature know Theo's thoughts? But more importantly, he couldn't believe a being as cruel and heartless as Lord Vodnik was on their side. Had he purposefully let Sly know what was going on so he could tell Theo?

The leader of the Vodni chuckled, his big belly rolling. "*Of course. Did you think I didn't know Sly was trailing me?*"

Magda slapped the creature hard. "This is no laughing matter."

She turned her hard glare in the direction Lord Vodnik stared. Then, it was her turn to stand dumbfounded. Finally, she shouted, "Traitor! Youdi, kill her!" Magda pointed toward Lamia.

Lamia paled. "You wanted to draw out Zlo. I know the one thing he needs." She snatched Pavel's sword to his astonished "Hey" and rushed toward her adversaries.

The Youdi were upon her in moments, striking, slicing, and stabbing since their magic was ineffective. Lamia did nothing to deter them. She had the full power of the ouroboros. She had Pavel's sword that repelled any evil intent directed at the carrier. And yet, she let the Youdi overpower her. It was almost as if … Theo couldn't complete the unbelievable thought.

"We have to help her." He rushed forward, his sword drawn.

Before he reached Lamia, the sky thundered. A black mist swirled above, forming into a man. Zlo. "Stop, you fools! I need her!"

Theo stopped in his tracks. Lamia had let herself be slaughtered so Zlo would reveal himself. Theo wouldn't let another sacrifice be in vain. Lamia had redeemed herself with her selfless act.

Zlo swooped down and cradled Lamia in his arms as he rose to the sky again. "Why did you do it? I offered you the world."

"You offered me slavery."

With trembling hands, Lamia unhooked the twin ouroboros belts and let them fall. Soon after they left her body, she dissolved into golden dust, leaving Zlo's arms empty. As the belts twirled to the ground, they burst into red and blue flames, symbolic of Zmey's fire and Lamia's hail that wrought destruction on the land.

"No!" Zlo screamed. He began to transform into a black mist to return to the void he'd come from. The beast's burning red eyes fixed on Theo. A twisted grin spread across Zlo's face. "You haven't seen the last of me. I'll find a way. I'll corrupt you or your sister or a future ruler from your line. You will never be free of me."

"Oh, yes, we will." Theo was ready. His own sacrifice would make Zmeykovo safe. "Light will overpower darkness. Prepare for Tangra to devour you."

Fear showed in Zlo's eyes as Theo's sword began to glow.

Chapter 19
Light and Darkness

ALL FIGHTING IN THE AIR and on the ground ceased. As Theo's power grew, he sensed the emotions of every man and beast alike. Friend and foe watched in anticipation, some curious, others fearful about the outcome of the imminent confrontation. Other fighters slipped away, knowing they were no longer needed. The strongest emotion came from Zlo, now a pair of red eyes amid a swirling black mass. Theo didn't fear his enemy's escape this time. The power to restrain the monster lay within Theo's ability.

"*Dragon spirit,*" he thought. "*I'm ready.*"

He no longer needed to speak to his dragon spirit. They were one. The wisdom of the ages poured into Theo. A more powerful dragon had never existed. He summoned the wind and rain with a flick of his hands. A cold, freezing gale blew in, encircling Zlo, keeping him stationary.

Zlo's silent screams and probing mind tried to batter Theo's consciousness. "*You can't do this. You're a failure. You're weak.*"

This time, Theo didn't fall prey to the evil lord's thought suggestions. Theo smiled instead. Then, keeping his eyes steady on the evil lord, Theo added fire to the wind and rain. Not any fire, but dragon fire. Rattan had said it would destroy or refine. Theo would command it to do both. He didn't even have to breathe the fire from his human form. The sword and his dragon spirit gave him the power to *think* the flames into existence. Flickers of the deadly light darted in and out of the swirling mass. Zlo screamed at the intensity of the inferno that consumed him, reshaped him for what was to come.

Even dragon fire was not enough. To obliterate the monster lurking within the darkness once and for all, Theo had to call forth every power imbued within the sword.

As he touched each symbol on the weapon, he spoke his words loud enough so all could hear.

"I now harness the fire of the Firebird." That symbol blazed red, and blood-red flames circled the sword.

"I draw forth the cyclical powers of the moon." The invoked symbol pulsed blue, and icy-blue flames joined the red in the dance.

"I pull from the sun its heavenly rays." The final symbol flashed a blinding white, and searing white flames completed the trilogy.

In the sky, the black mass that was Zlo beat against the elements holding him in place. His words were a jumble of shrieks and oaths. No one besides Theo gave the evil lord a glance. All eyes were peeled to the powerful being holding the sword aloft.

Theo closed his eyes. Not because of the intensity of the light, but because the moment had arrived. Once he continued with the ritual, stopping would be impossible, despite the consequences he could suffer. He breathed deeply to calm himself and took a moment to recall his life, however short it had been.

Scenes from Selo sped past. A young boy's lifetime of hard work. He had tried to be the man of the family. Grief had never left his mother for her husband lost at sea. His sister, Nia, had battled him on many occasions. Her strong will rebelled against being bossed around. A tear trickled down Theo's face. He loved them both so much.

Next, Pavel's face flashed before Theo's eyes. The two of them had gone on adventure after adventure. Many scrapes, bruises, and scoldings couldn't keep the friends from seeking the secrets of the world.

Finally, Zmeykovo appeared. Theo's heart broke. Not for himself, but for those who lived here. He had thought his life in a small village had been difficult, but here … so much injustice thrived. So many wrongs existed that Theo wanted to right.

He took one more long breath and opened his eyes, fixing them on Zlo. The first step in restoring Zmeykovo was returning that monster to the place he belonged.

It was time.

Theo raised the sword higher. The red, blue, and white flames wove together like a rope, tightening around the weapon. They spun faster and faster, a blur of colors becoming violet. The light traveled to the hilt. Then farther. They crept up Theo's arms and down his body until he shone with a violet hue.

Theo and the sword became one.

Power like nothing he'd ever felt before filled him. He didn't need the apple. He could conquer the world now if he chose. But that was not his desire. The world could be a beautiful place if those with the power to change it used it for good. He couldn't understand why so many did the opposite.

The power was invigorating. He felt like a seed growing into a seedling, longing to push his head into the world beyond to see what wonders and beauties lay there. Perhaps when he accomplished his task at hand, the world just beyond his reach would be made known to him. A new life. He felt its pull.

"I am a candle, a light to dispel the darkness," he shouted. "Tangra! I am ready."

A deafening roar reverberated through the sky, and a flaming chariot, pulled by two magnificent golden horses, descended from the heavens.

Zlo's "No!" forced its way out of the dark mist and echoed along with the heavenly thunder.

Along the path where Tangra drove his chariot, the sky split open. A chasm as dark as a black hole was surrounded by a blinding white.

Sparks flew from the swirling black mist. Zlo scratched and clawed against his restraints to find a way out of his prison. But the elements held him bound. The dragon fire struck time and again, slowly refining the creature within.

Theo called on the power of the moon. With a forceful mental thrust, he hurled the swirling black mass that was Zlo into the darkness. Out in that world beyond, the dragon fire would continue its refining process until every spec with an evil trace was burned clean of impurities. The atoms would spread far and wide. Eons would pass before they found each other again and could reunite, if ever. Out there, uninhibited by the influences of

Earthly beings, a new creature could be reshaped, one devoid of any semblance of Lord Zlo.

Theo connected with Zlo's mind. *"You wanted to open a portal to the human world to wreak your destruction. Tangra chose another portal for you, one where you can do no harm."*

The evil lord had already undergone too much transformation from the dragon fire to respond. All that Theo could discern from the black mist was a weak whimper.

He sighed in relief that the reign of terror was over. The light could chase away the darkness for a time, but could never wipe it from existence completely. Both light and darkness were necessities, but the darkness did not have to be evil.

When Zlo was far beyond the ability to return to this world, Tangra rode his chariot away, and the sky closed like a zipper. Theo watched the departure until the Thracian god became one with the sun. The sky returned to a pale blue, and the sun shone upon the scene below as if nothing out of the ordinary had happened.

A stunned silence filled the fortress courtyard and beyond. No cheers. No angry shouts. The moment was too overwhelming for anyone to react. Everyone simply slipped away back to the life they had led before. To think about all that had transpired. Some to later rejoice. Others to be thankful they had survived the new dragon king's wrath.

Power seeped out of Theo, and his body lost its glow. The violet light in the sword untangled into its three strands, each retreating into the symbol from which it had come. Theo held his breath and waited.

Nothing happened.

The sword's power hadn't consumed him the way he had expected. To keep the balance of nature. He turned around and wrapped his arms around both Diva and Pavel.

"I'm here. I'm still alive!"

Pavel pulled away, surprise and anger on his face. "What do you mean? Did you do this thinking it would kill you?" He beat his fists against Theo's chest. "I could kill you for that."

Diva gave Theo's arm a squeeze. He was certain she understood and would have done the same.

"Okay, that's enough." She pulled Pavel away. "Theo did what had to be done."

"I know, but … but …" Pavel burst into tears and squeezed Theo tight. "Don't ever do anything like that again."

"I seriously hope I don't have to."

The three of them stood in silence. Alone. Looking at all the destruction. Why did people have to cause so much hurt? Was power that important? What did it gain anyone that they couldn't achieve in more beneficial ways? Theo felt good about himself when he helped others. How could some people feel good about themselves for their selfish wants?

After a moment, Diva said, "The threat is over, but we should find the Golden Apple and get it back to the Colobari. They'll know what to do to protect it from anyone else wanting its power."

"Like Magda," Theo replied.

"Oh, speaking of her," Pavel said as he dug inside his backpack. "I have something you might like." He pulled out a medallion that looked like Theo's and handed it to him.

"What?" Theo tilted his head and raised his eyebrows. "How did you get that?"

"Funny story. Well, kinda funny." Pavel pushed his glasses up the bridge of his nose. "I still had your invisible scarf." He looked once more in his backpack and handed the scarf to Theo. "So, when you found out where Magda was, I put the scarf back on and snuck over there."

"You did what?" Theo shouted. "Invisible or not, you were in danger. Magda might have detected you."

Pavel scowled. "After what you just did and the danger you put yourself in, don't even think about scolding me for anything I do."

"I ... I ..."

"Anyway, it was nothing to worry about." Pavel shrugged. "All the other excitement with Lamia and Zlo happened while I snuck over to the watchtower. By the time I got there, Magda had already fled."

"Then how did you get her medallion?" Theo asked.

"Lord Vodnik had somehow managed to get it off her undetected."

"And ..." Theo asked when Pavel paused for way too long.

"Oh, yah." Pavel smirked. "He said it was payment for his services to her."

"So, what he was saying was that he stole it."

Pavel nodded. "Anyway, he didn't want to give it to me, even for a trade, so I tossed the silver net over him. He howled and grumbled for a while before he threw the medallion out. I grabbed it and left."

"Did you take the net off of him?"

"Nah. I thought I'd let him stew for a while," Pavel replied. "I didn't trust him not to try to get the medallion back. I'm sure someone helped him later. Plenty of his children were here."

Diva grinned the whole time. "Maybe they didn't remove it either. He is rather cruel to them."

Theo looked at the medallion. Now he had a chance to see what it said. The words "Born to Rule" were written in the same type of runes that were on Theo's medallion.

"No wonder Magda had such an obsession with being the ruler of the Samodivi." He shook his head. "Her medallion told her that it was her destiny."

Theo passed the medallion to Diva. "Magda told me these were twin gifts. I have mine. This one should be yours. And who is better to rule Zmeykovo than you?"

Without saying anything, Diva took the medallion. A sparkling light shot up her fingertips and lit her hand for a brief moment. She took a step back and fumbled with the medallion, but kept hold of it.

"Whoa, what was that?" Pavel asked.

"I don't know." Diva waited a moment longer before she put it around her neck. "It feels warm."

Pavel touched the medallion, but nothing happened. He stopped and stared. "Diva, look at your palm!"

She looked. Where she had held the medallion, a new tattoo had formed, bearing the same words: Born to Rule.

"Just like what my medallion did." Theo rubbed the spot on his chest where the words "Unborn Hero" had been branded on him. They had faded somewhat over time, but he could still read the words. "It definitely has some connection to you."

She said nothing but gave Theo's arm another squeeze.

The three of them walked into the fortress in search of the Golden Apple. From time to time, one of them or the other broke out in giggles, thinking about Lord Vodnik wrapped up in the silver net, struggling like a fish to get out.

Then they grew serious as they surveyed the hallways, searching for anyone who might still be loyal to either Lamia or Zlo. But they met no confrontations. The fortress was eerily quiet. Their footsteps echoed as Diva led them down various passageways deeper into the fortress. Her memory of where she had been held during her kidnapping had apparently returned.

"Here." Diva stopped in front of a wooden door.

Nothing set it aside as being different from any of the others they had passed along the way. She opened it without effort. No magic barred her way. If there had been any before, Lamia's death had ensured the magic returned to the elements from which it came.

Diva stepped inside, followed by Theo and Pavel.

"Wow! Look at that." Pavel pointed to a painting on the wall opposite them.

Soft amber light in the bedroom highlighted a portrait of Zmey and Lamia in human appearance. The two of them held their smiling faces close together, like modern-day people taking a selfie. Lamia must have taken the painting with her from the castle at some point.

When? Theo probably would never know. It could have been when she was young. But then, why would it be here? Lamia and Zlo hadn't occupied Kaleto Fortress until after she'd been resurrected. She must have gone back to the castle and retrieved it. Despite all her denials about having any affection for Zmey, she had been lying. A part of her must have always wanted to make things return to the way they had been when she was a youth.

"Diva, do you think I could have helped her?" he silently asked.

"No, she was too far under Zlo's influence," Diva replied. *"Helping her would have only doomed you."*

Out loud, Diva said, "It's so sad they spent most of their lives fighting each other."

"It is." This time it was Theo's turn to squeeze Diva's arm, letting her know that they wouldn't be like that. It was better not to think about that now and continue with why they came here. "Do you know where Lamia would have put the Golden Apple?"

"No. When I was here before, it was on the bureau."

"Hey, how about this?" Pavel had been exploring the room. He pointed to a dragon decoration on the stone wall. Green gemstone eyes sparkled in the room's dim light.

Theo and Diva came closer, and she touched one of the eyes.

The wall behind the dragon opened with heavy scraping across the floor.

"Amazing!" Pavel peered inside. "This closet would make Nia green with envy."

Maybe the way Nia had been before, Theo thought to himself.

After her own abduction by Lamia and narrowly escaping being a sacrifice, Nia had changed. She'd matured quickly. Theo hoped she and his human mother were getting on fine without him. With the Zmeykovo adventure nearing its end, he and Pavel would be returning to Selo soon. Theo sighed, not sure he wanted that. Zmeykovo now had Diva to make it run smoothly. Once more, Theo didn't know where he belonged.

He shoved aside his thoughts and looked into the massive hidden closet. Glamorous dresses, shoes, and jewelry filled the racks and shelves. Diva searched along the far end of a shelf and dragged an object forward.

"Here it is." She lifted the box that held the Golden Apple.

Theo breathed a sigh of relief. He didn't have to open the box to know the real apple was inside. Its power still called to him.

"Let's get this back to the Colobari," he said. "They'll know what to do with it."

Chapter 20
Dragon Legacy

THEO WASN'T SURPRISED to find the Colobari waiting for him back at the castle. He was glad. He wanted nothing more than to be rid of the box that held the Golden Apple. The sooner the better. The priests should *purify* the apple. Its continued existence to tempt anyone else in Zmeykovo was a danger.

At the harvesting ceremony, when one of the priests had approached Kosara, she'd told him Bendis wanted a different ritual performed. Well, nothing of that sort had happened. Instead, Magda had stolen the apple and set off a chain reaction of destruction.

Why hadn't Bendis and Tangra allowed Kosara to perform the ritual in the first place? Kosara had said only the first Golden Apple had ever been consumed, and it had resulted in massacres. Surely, they didn't want that to happen again? They knew that was Zlo's plan. It would have made much more sense to purify the apple right away so it lost its power.

What else had Kosara said? Theo thought back to the harvesting ritual. Something about the Thracian deities had determined that he was worthy and almost ready. Ready for what?

"We see you have questions." Kobur the Eagle approached and bowed. "And we are ready to answer them."

"Why didn't you perform a ritual on the apple when you had a chance?" Theo said out loud, even though the Colobari already knew his thoughts.

"Wise observation," Kobur replied. "It was the only way to ensure Zlo's removal. We had every faith that you would achieve this."

Now Theo was really confused. He'd thought the reason he hadn't transported the real Golden Apple to the castle was a test to make sure he didn't fall prey to the fruit's power. Zmey had said that wasn't so. That the real apple had been brought to the castle in secret because it would attract too many power-hungry people. Had the Colobari not told Zmey the entire story?

"I don't get it." Theo shook his head. "You knew all along this would happen?"

"Knew? No. It was one of many possibilities," Kobur said. "We put our trust in you that the most favorable outcome would occur."

Theo's head spun. Instead of testing him, the Colobari had seen that he'd send Zlo off into another dimension. "What else did you see that could have happened?"

Kobur glanced at Diva, then back at Theo.

Oh, no. Theo's heart raced. *They didn't see Diva becoming evil and eating the apple, did they?*

She elbowed him and said out loud, "Never in a million years."

Theo had momentarily forgotten Diva could share his thoughts if he didn't guard them.

"What did I miss?" Pavel asked.

"Nothing." Theo repeated his question. "What were some other possibilities?"

"One serious one involved your sister," Kobur said.

Again, Theo's heart clenched.

"We saw the need to use the Golden Apple to revive her."

Theo breathed a sigh of relief, and Diva said in his mind, "*Told you.*"

No other outcome mattered now to Theo. If the Colobari had seen that the Golden Apple might be needed to save Diva, then he was glad they hadn't purified it.

"Here." Theo handed the box to Kobur. "Please do something with it now to make it safe. You'll have to remove the enchantment on the box, though. Magda put some kind of spell on it so Lamia couldn't open it."

Kobur ran his hand over the box. "This is nothing more than a weak beginner's charm. Magda never fulfilled her potential. Too much darkness lay in her heart to become a priestess of Tangra."

Theo raised his eyebrows. Two things raced through his mind. First, Magda had said she'd studied to be the first woman Colobar, but Tangra had rejected her. She had never said exactly why, but his aunt had made it sound as if Zunitza and Zmey were responsible for the rejection. Instead, Magda's failure was her own fault. It made her cold. She harbored too much hatred and jealousy to serve a deity who brought warmth and light to the world.

Second, Theo couldn't help but wonder about the powers of the Colobari. Kobur said the spell Magda conjured was weak. Yet, from what Theo had seen, his aunt was second only to Baba Yaga as far as witches went. At least Baba Yaga claimed to be the "witch of witches." If Lamia and Zlo couldn't undo Magda's *weak* spell, then the Colobari themselves had to have powers beyond comprehension.

"Can't you just destroy the apple?" Pavel spoke up. "I think we've all had enough of it."

Theo and Diva both nodded.

"No," Kobur said. "To do so would cause the Firebird's death. Their existence is intertwined, since the purpose of the Firebird is to protect the apple until it is harvested. When the Firebird dies and is reborn, a new apple grows. So, too, when the apple is destroyed or consumed, the Firebird ceases to exist and must be reborn."

Theo sensed a sad story must exist behind that revelation. He'd look the tale up in the *Lodge* book if the Colobari left it in the library. Somehow, he felt they'd secure the book elsewhere now.

"Even when it's used for healing?" he asked.

"Even then."

Theo sighed. "Do you have all the Golden Apples from the past stored away somewhere safe?"

Kobur shook his head. "There is no need for that. When the Firebird is reborn naturally every thousand years, the previous apple turns to dust."

"So there's always an apple in the Chamber Room, except when it's growing?" Theo asked.

"This is true. Except when someone steals it."

Just great. That threat would always hang over Zmeykovo. At least when this apple's power was neutralized, there would be no imminent danger.

"It doesn't seem safe to keep it there," Theo said. "Look how easy it was for Magda to get in. All she had to do was take Zmey's key when he was unconscious. Isn't there some other place to guard the apple?"

"Under normal circumstances, the keeper of the key would know the room had been breached," Kobur said. "Or we would have. We stand guard over it at all times, except when the king summons us. In this case, Magda used another ability she learned when she trained to be a Colobar. She masked her presence in the room while we were in consultation with your father. This failure will not happen again."

Pavel snorted. "Zmey keeps the door locked. You can't possibly be in the room all the time."

"I think they can," Theo said. "They're bird statues in the room. And they change to this form when Zmey calls them."

"This is true." Kobur handed Theo the key he'd seen around Zmey's neck. The key that opened the door to the Chamber Room. "That legacy now belongs to you. You may seek our advice at any time."

Theo gulped. So much responsibility. "How … how did you get this?"

"When the holder of the key dies, the key returns to us, so we may present it to the heir."

Reluctantly, Theo took the key and placed the chain around his neck. "I will do my best."

"I have no doubt you will," Kobur said, and the three Colobari bowed to him and crossed their staffs. "We shall take the apple to Kosara for now. When we return, we will teach you the sacred knowledge necessary to both restore us to our guardian form and to recall us when you need assistance. Fare thee well, Dragon King."

With that, the Colobari departed for the Znahar Tree.

Being called the dragon king struck Theo hard. His father was truly gone. This responsibility now lay on his shoulders. And Diva's. She was the queen of Zmeykovo, and also the queen of the Samodivi. All she needed was …

"Zunitza's crown! We have to find it," he said. "We have both parts of the medallion now, but we don't know where the crown is. I have to find out from Zunitza."

Diva smiled. "Don't bother her. I know where it is. Follow me."

She led them to the small ballroom and stood in front of the statue of Zmey and Lamia's parents.

"Remember how I had a vision of Zunitza when I touched the statue?" she said. "I'm sure the crown is hidden in there."

Theo removed his medallion from around his neck and Diva did the same with the one she had been given.

"Magda said they are more powerful together," Theo said. "So how do we join them?"

"Remember, yours has that tiny bump on the outside." Diva examined the one she held. "And mine has an indent in the same location. That must connect them."

She handed her medallion to Theo, and he snapped them together. Nothing happened. Theo moaned. He wasn't sure what he had expected. A flash of light, at least.

"Now what?" he asked. "If you think the crown is inside the statue, how do we use this to get it?"

"I'm not sure. We'll have to look all around the statue," Diva said.

"While you two do that," Pavel said, "I'm going to look at those cool dragon figures on that even cooler fireplace."

The fireplace was magnificent, with its smooth black fieldstone surface and three openings at angles to each other. Golden stones shaped like scales covered the entire wall behind the fireplace.

"Haven't you already looked at them?" Theo asked.

The way to the hidden library lay behind the wall. Pushing the third statue from the left backward opened a secret passageway. Theo had led Diva and Pavel through there when they'd gone to the library. The underground passages twisted and turned, certain to confuse anyone not familiar with them. When the Colobari had met with the others to strategize in the library, the men had marked the passages to make it easier for everyone to find the way, since the library no longer needed to remain hidden.

"Nah, we were in too much of a hurry."

Pavel ran a commentary as he examined the figures. "This one's flying. Neat, these two are fighting." On and on he went, while Theo and Diva searched for where to place the merged medallions.

"I don't see anything. Do you, Diva?"

"Not a thing."

"Here." Theo handed her the medallions. "You saw Zunitza the last time. Maybe if you hold them and touch the statue again, you'll know where they go."

Diva took them and placed her hand on the statues. Nothing happened. She held the medallions against each statue and the two eggs, one at a time. The statue remained immobile and silent.

"There has to be a way." Theo ran his fingers through his hair, while Pavel prattled on about dragon statues.

"Hey, look at this one. It's a miniature version of the big statue." Pavel touched it, and the statue tilted backward.

A creaking noise came from what Theo called the "dragons in love" statue. The eggs between the two dragons slid aside, like opening doors, revealing a star shape beneath each of them.

"Pavel, you did it," Theo shouted. "Come on back and watch while we see what happens."

Pavel scrambled over to his friends.

"I guess the medallions don't belong together." Theo unsnapped them and handed Diva back hers.

He peered at the star shapes on the statue. "Mine looks like it goes under Zmey's egg, so yours must fit under Lamia's."

Theo placed his medallion over the star shape, and Diva did the same.

A vibrating energy filled the room. It surged through Theo's body. He sensed Diva react as it filled her, too. The medallions glowed, and a beam of light shot out of each of them. It twisted together as it pointed back to the statue. The dragons moved apart, revealing a hidden compartment in the base below the eggs.

Theo started to put his hand into the crevice without looking, but stopped. The last time he'd done that, he'd been bitten by a snake. He crouched onto the floor and peered inside. A violet velvet pouch, with a golden cord lay on top of a book.

"I think the crown's in there." Theo pulled out the pouch and handed it to Diva. He next retrieved the book, made sure nothing else was inside the compartment, and stood. "I wonder what this says."

An image of a dragon holding two eggs, one gold and one white, decorated the cover of the leather-bound tome. He opened it, and a piece of parchment fluttered to the floor. Theo bent to retrieve it.

"It's a letter."

"Magda and Zunitza probably left each other notes," Pavel said. "I want to see the crown."

With trembling hands, Diva opened the pouch and removed a crown with golden leaves that twisted around the headband and hung in long chains down the side. This was the crown Theo had seen in the painting in Zmey's den, the day Kosara's messengers came to tell him the Golden Apple was ready for harvesting.

Diva drew in a long breath. "It's more beautiful than its pictures. Books say that Bendis crafted it for our queen."

"You should try it on," Pavel said.

"Oh no." Diva replaced it in the pouch. "This belongs only to a queen."

Theo placed a hand on her arm. "*You* are the Samodivi queen now."

Diva's cheeks turned red, and tears threatened to spill down her cheeks. "I can't possibly wear it until an official ceremony. What does the letter say?"

Theo knew she didn't want to talk about her new role now. But he was curious what the letter contained, too. He didn't think it was some youthful letter exchanged between sisters. He began to read.

Beloved future twins,

I have had a vision of twins being born to twins. You two from the future are destined to save the kingdom during the most catastrophic time our land has ever known. Beautiful twin girls have been born among the Samodivi this day. I have also seen that one of them will give birth to you, our heroic twins, yet I know not which sister it will be. You, my beloved grandchildren, shall continue the royal line, for my son, Zmey, will fall in love with and marry one of these Samodivi twins.

When these lovely girls reach the proper age of marriage, I shall explain to them what I have seen. I leave with each Samodiva twin a special token given to all royal twins. These shall be yours when you are born.

One of you will bear the title of "Unborn Hero," while the other the message of "Born to Rule," for she—I know one of the children will be a girl—will become the queen, not only of Zmeykovo, but also of the Samodivi. The gender of the other child is hidden from me. Both of you will be strong and brave, and your love for each other and your land will be enduring.

Take heart and protect Zmeykovo with your love. This is your legacy. Use this journal to document your journey together and treasure it and tell it to future generations.

Fondly yours,
Hala, your devoted grandmother

Theo wiped away tears. Magda had lied about the twin medallions. Or hadn't told the entire story. They had been meant for him and Diva all along, not Magda and Zunitza. His mother didn't die because she had given the medallion to Theo. Her death hadn't transferred the power and title to him. The destiny to become the Unborn Hero had always belonged to him.

Now it made more sense why Magda had wanted to marry Zmey, so her children would be rulers. Theo couldn't help but wonder if his aunt would have found a way to dispose of her own twins, so that she could continue to rule. She was so power hungry that it was unlikely she would have wanted to share it with her own children.

He looked at the letter again. Hala must have written this before she herself became corrupt. The Golden Apple had consumed her when Zmey and Lamia were older, and at some point, Lamia had killed her own mother.

Diva took his hand. For several moments, they stood in silence. Words were unnecessary as they shared thoughts about the past and wondered about the future. Could they bring a golden age to Zmeykovo? Had Hala seen peace in the land under his and Diva's rule?

Chapter 21
Long Live the Queen

JULY 27

FROM ALL OVER ZMEYKOVO, residents and animals congregated around Samodivi Lake. Today was a joyous day, unlike the last time they had gathered here. Diva was not lying near death. She was about to be crowned queen of the Samodivi and co-ruler of Zmeykovo in a joint ceremony.

The setting sun painted the golden water with rosy hues. The hum of voices and the sounds of nature set a soothing stage for the upcoming event. Willow branches and wildflowers decorated a platform that had been set up at the shoreline. Their sweet scent perfumed the air. Birds stayed up late to sing their joyous songs for the one who cared for their needs, their beloved new queen.

Theo tugged at his fancy royal clothing, adorned with jewels and gold, as he paced along the beach. "Ugh. This shirt is too stiff and formal," he said to Boo, who hopped alongside.

At least he was allowed to carry his sword with him. The threat of Lamia and Zlo had been eliminated, but Magda and other traitors like Radan, Bor Stobor, and the Knights of Darkness still roamed free.

"Your clothes don't seem that bad," the magpie replied.

Theo snorted. "Easy for you to say. You get to wear feathers all the time."

"And fine feathers they are." Boo stopped to preen. "Stop fidgeting. You have to look the part of a ruler as you greet your subjects."

Subjects. Theo shivered at the word. He'd never expected he'd have to take over the kingdom so soon. He wanted to grieve for his father, but he'd been kept too busy since the battle. He couldn't believe that it had been only a little more than a week ago.

"I wonder how much longer before Diva gets here."

Theo now regretted that he'd volunteered to come to the lake early to greet everyone. He'd hoped that Diva would be with him, but Ula and Sava had said they needed time alone with Diva. So, here he was, pacing the beach, when he should be talking with everyone.

Boo pecked at Theo's shoes. "Stop wasting time. You don't want to disappoint Diva, do you?"

"No, I guess not." Theo sighed and strode toward the crowd.

He looked for Pavel. There he was, still by the food table, where he had deserted Theo the moment they arrived at the lake. He wasn't going to get much help from Pavel in socializing. Theo had to go it alone.

Before he'd taken more than a few steps, Baba Yaga quietly—and smokelessly—flew in.

"See you later, Theo." Boo squawked and flew away. The magpie resented Baba Yaga for kidnapping him and then giving him to the Youdi. It would be a long time before he forgave her, if ever.

The witch set her wooden mortar down in front of Theo and hopped out. "Ah, perfect landing. Much easier to navigate my old Chutura than that newfangled one."

Kikimora poked her head out. "And much safer, too, I must say."

Theo shook his head. "What happened to the new vehicle? You complained to Diva for so long about not getting it. Then the Samodivi had Sitara hurry up and finish your fancy one. And now you're back to your old one. And why doesn't it puff out that black smoke anymore?"

"So many questions. Couldn't get used to all those gadgets." She glanced at Kiki who was trying to crawl out of the mortar. In a whisper, Baba Yaga said, "Lesnik said he'd fix my faithful old Chutura if I didn't tell Kiki where he was hiding out. Kiki's better off without him, don't you think?"

Theo nodded. For once, he agreed with the witch. "Thank you for coming." The words stuck in his throat. Baba Yaga had done some good deeds, but he still held resentments toward her.

"Oh, so you're finally going to be nice to me?" She grinned, showing her green gums and iron teeth. "I guess Lord Vodnik made you see sense. You can't keep hating me when I had no control over what Zlo wanted."

"What do you mean?" When had the swamp creature talked to Theo about Baba Yaga?

Then Theo understood. Lord Vodnik had been able to read Theo's thoughts during the battle. The swamp menace had said something about no one saying no to a witch. But there was something more. He'd said a witch greater than Magda had people she couldn't deny. The only witch who claimed to be the "witch of witches" was Baba Yaga.

Theo stared at her with his mouth open. "You gave him the ability to read my mind? How could you?"

"Oh, pft." She waved her hand in a dismissive manner. "It was only temporary so he could get my message to you. I thought you might believe someone else telling you what I've tried to say."

"I … I …" He wasn't sure how to process that information.

"Besides that, he came to me asking for help." She stared at Theo with an accusing eye. "All you folks only stop by when you want something. Only Kiki visits with no expectations."

"Maybe because you always threaten to eat people." Theo rolled his eyes. "And what did Lord Vodnik want?"

"A spell to make his suffocating water ineffective in case Sly didn't get the message to you."

Now, Theo stood with his mouth open. He couldn't believe Lord Vodnik had made that request. Finally, Theo said, "And what was your price for helping? And what was Lord Vodnik expecting to get out of it? Neither one of you does anything for free."

Baba Yaga snorted. "Not true. I did it for nothing in return. You're no Zmey, but maybe time will change that. And Lord Vodnik said he'd steal … get something from Magda."

"I … I …" Once more, Theo didn't know what to say.

"I accept your apology."

"I wasn't—"

"Shh." Baba Yaga leaned closer, gagging Theo with her bad breath. "If you look at the edge of the forest, you'll see Lord

Vodnik and Lesnik. Les couldn't come all the way, you know." She gestured toward Kiki. "But they both wanted to thank you."

Theo looked where the witch pointed. Two sets of green hands waved, one covered with leaves and twigs and the other with moss from the swamp. Theo waved back.

"Okay," Baba Yaga said. "Now that that's settled, here." She thrust a vial into his hands. "A gift from me for our new queen. Long may she reign. It's a healing potion with herbs found only in my garden."

Kikimora had managed to get out of the mortar by then. "Hello, my handsome boy." She fluttered her eyelids at him. "So happy you're staying. I have a gift for you and our new queen, too." She handed over two brown bottles. "My newest brew, made in honor of our new king and queen."

"Thank you. Thank you, both." It was time to get into host mode. "There's plenty of food. Help yourselves."

As they walked away, Theo chuckled to himself. *That will serve Pavel right for abandoning me for food. When he sees Kikimora, he'll run away.*

A screech followed, and Pavel tore away toward the beach. Theo had hoped by now Sirin's song would have lessened the effects of the nightmares Pavel had about Kikimora. After all the horrors and nasty creatures they'd encountered, she was the one who still terrified his friend the most. Perhaps with more time, Pavel's dread would lessen.

Pavel slowed as he approached Theo. "Oh, hey. There you are. I was looking for you."

"Right." Theo nodded. "Want to go see Sitara and Jega with me?"

"Sure."

They walked and chatted with friends and those they hadn't met before. Theo felt more secure with Pavel by his side. It was funny how now that the worst danger was over, Theo reverted to his shy self. Pavel, however, had no problem talking with anyone. Each guest presented Theo gifts, handmade items that reflected that person's profession: cheeses, soaps, iron and wooden household implements, weapons, clothing, and more.

Some items were for both him and Diva, others special gifts for their beloved new queen. Sitara had made Diva a golden comb and mirror, encrusted with gems. Jega had made her the softest pair of leather boots. Drakus had foraged into the depths of the demon forest and gathered seeds from magical plants few dared to venture there to find. And Jabalaka, with Sly by his side, had rebound a copy of the entire history of Zmeykovo for her. Even Sly said he had a gift that was waiting back at the castle. His father had allowed Sly to give the royal family the water bull, Lucky, who had played a vital role in one adventure.

Mraz, the eldest of the Kukeri brothers, had returned from hiding, now that the threat of anyone gaining control of *Lamia's Bible* had been eliminated. The Kuker gave Theo a wooden mask, covered with animal skins. Thankfully, it wasn't as terrifying as the ones he'd seen the men wear the first time he'd met them.

"We have all made you an honorary member of the Kukeri," Mraz said. "Your bravery and care of Zmeykovo have earned you that right."

Theo hugged his friend, glad that he had remained safe.

After that, Theo and Pavel had to make several trips to deposit the gifts onto a table set up for that purpose.

Vodna and the Rusalki stayed out in the lake, sitting on boulders or splashing in the water, but Theo's friend Ruslana swam ashore and presented him with her queen's gift, the kaval that had once belonged to his mother.

"Vodna was reluctant to part with this," Ruslana said, "but she appreciates everything you've done to save Zmeykovo. If you ever need another favor from her, though, she'll want it back."

"Thank you." Theo hugged the musical instrument to his chest. This more than made up for the Rusalki's lack of support during Zlo's reign of terror. He faced the water and bowed to the queen of the Rusalki, and she lowered her head in acknowledgement.

By the time Theo and Pavel had made the rounds, Theo's arms and voice box were sore, but he was smiling. It was wonderful to have people relaxed again. Their lives could get back to normal.

Dusk had nearly fallen by the time they'd finished visiting guests.

Theo plopped down onto the beach, and Pavel joined him.

"You know, we're going to have to go back to Selo soon," Theo said. "The portals are all open now and safe to travel."

Pavel sighed. "I know. I miss my family, but ..."

Theo knew exactly what his friend was feeling. "I get ya. It's like this is the real world and home is some kind of fantasy."

"Yes!" Pavel shouted. "Exactly that. Only ..." His face became sad. "You belong here, and I don't."

"That's not true." Theo rapped Pavel's shoulder. "You've done a lot to save Zmeykovo. Everyone accepts you, accepts both of us. We'll make it work somehow. Here and in Selo. Both of us together."

"She's coming!" someone yelled.

Theo glanced toward the direction of Cherna Mountain. Soft green glows flickered in the sky from Sur's herd as they and their Samodivi riders escorted Diva to the lake. Their new queen rode at the front, with the herd on either side. The Samodivi who were on the ground formed two lines and created a tunnel by joining their raised hands.

"That's your signal to go up on stage," Pavel said.

Theo sighed. He hated the formality, but he'd do it for Diva. He joined the Colobari, who were present to officiate the ceremony.

Most of the deer landed. Twelve remained in the air, flying over the platform. Wreaths of wildflowers decorated the animals' necks. But Theo paid more attention to his sister. Diva's wild, curly hair sparkled from the glow of torches set up along the beach. Sur marched with strong, steady steps toward the platform. When he reached the tunnel created by the Samodivi, he stopped and Diva slid off of his back. She hugged her deer companion.

Sava, Ula, and the other Samodivi who had landed dismounted as well. They lined up along both sides of Diva, and then the entourage proceeded. Diva stepped through the tunnel, while the others walked along the outside. When Diva exited the other end at the steps of the platform, the Samodivi released their hands. A soft, gentle melody began to play. Theo couldn't tell where it came from. It seemed to originate from every corner of the forest, every grain of sand along the beach, and every drop of water in the lake. Nature itself was singing.

Standing by the Colobari, he smiled at his sister. Her pale face had flushed, but her eyes sparkled. He reached out a hand toward her, and she flowed up the steps to stand beside him.

A shower of flower petals fell around them. Theo looked up. The deer above them had formed a circle. They beat their wings in perfect unison as they flew around the platform. The Samodivi riders sang as they tossed down petals of every color of the rainbow. Cheers came from those gathered on the ground and in the water.

As the last petal landed, Theo and Diva turned their attention to Kobur the Eagle.

The words of the ceremony were a blur. When it came time for the Colobar to name Theo king, he was surprised at the lightness of the crown. Rattan the Hawk spoke to Theo's mind. *"The crown is not meant to be a burden, nor is the responsibility of ruling those in Zmeykovo. The role is to guide and assist, not to demand and control."*

Theo gave a slight bow with his head to acknowledge the wisdom of those words.

When Kobur placed the Samodiva crown upon Diva's head, Theo was mesmerized. An image of his mother—their mother—walking in a forest filled his mind. White butterflies fluttered around the queen of the Samodivi like gentle-falling snowflakes. The same crown that now sat upon Diva had adorned Zunitza. It was a natural extension of Diva's ethereal beauty. The golden leaves swayed, caressed by the breeze. The crown sparkled in the waning sunlight, a beacon of his sister's majesty and beauty.

So caught up in the scene, Theo almost missed it when Kobur held out a staff. Magic pulsed within the handle, and the head, in the shape of a dragon, held a slight glow. Kobur spoke about how it was to be used for good, for protection. To cause destruction or chaos would drain the wielder, not only of his own power, but of the light within his heart.

Theo's head spun with the responsibility. He couldn't help thinking if this was how it had been at first for Lamia and Zmey. Somewhere along the way, they had become enemies.

Diva squeezed his hand and thought to him, *"We're not like that. We'll keep each other safe and honest."*

Finally, the ceremony came to an end, with Kobur presenting Theo and Diva to the community as the king and queen of Zmeykovo, and Diva as the queen of the Samodivi.

The crowd cheered and tossed more flower petals into the air. Each Samodiva approached the platform and laid a small bouquet of rowan flowers at Diva's feet. "A symbol of our loyalty and devotion to you, our queen," they each said.

Sava and Ula came last and did the same. Diva and her sisters had tears of joy in their eyes. This was not a rivalry, but a celebration. The three of them hugged, and Diva said, "I may be your queen, but don't ever forget that you are my sisters, my family."

Although night had fallen, a rainbow glowed bright in the sky, its colors stretching across the forest and lake. Silver dust sparkled along its entirety. Everyone cheered once more. Zunitza and Zmey had come to add their blessing to the coronation of their children.

Hand-in-hand, Theo and Diva stepped off of the platform. Pavel had squeezed his way to the front. He held out a bouquet of beautiful wildflowers, decorated with washers dyed gold.

Theo gave Pavel a strange look, and Pavel thought back to the unasked question, *"I wanted to make it something that reflected me, and I didn't have much else here."*

To Diva, Pavel said as he bowed, "You look beautiful, my Queen."

Diva took the flowers and laughed. "They're lovely, but don't you ever call me that again. Friends don't give friends titles."

"You are beautiful." Theo gave her a hug. "Very royal."

"And so are you."

Theo fidgeted more in his clothing.

"I know how you feel," she said. "I prefer my simple robe and leather sandals. And I feel incomplete without my pouch and bow. You're lucky the Colobari let you wear your sword."

"I told them I refused to leave it back at the castle."

"Hey, both of you," Pavel said. "Stop complaining about your clothes. You can wear them for a special occasion like this. You can change later. Right now, let's get some food. I'm starving."

As they walked toward the food table, Theo said, "You know, in books, something always interrupts ceremonies like this before they can finish. I'm glad we made it through ours."

He had no sooner finished speaking when crashing came from the forest. Magda strode forward, followed by Radan, Zlo's second in command, Bor Stobor the Karakonjul, and the Knights of Darkness. No demons were present, though. Without the mind control of Lamia or Zlo, the demons had apparently deserted the rebellion.

Why didn't I keep my mouth shut? was the first thing that crossed Theo's mind. Next, he drew his sword, ready for battle.

Magda screeched, "I've come to claim what is mine! The crown." She shifted into a crow and flew straight for Diva.

Chapter 22
Magnificent Dragons

MAGDA THE CROW, with her claws extended, soared inches in front of Diva. Without thinking, Theo and Diva crossed the staffs the Colobari had presented them and pointed them toward their enemy. A beam of light shot out, hitting the crow and sending her tumbling backward.

Behind Magda, Radan, Bor Stobor, and the Knights of Darkness surged forward. Kukeri, Samodivi, Drakus, and Sitara whipped out weapons and took a stance. Nobody would get through their barricade.

A piercing power vibrated off of Magda as she spun in a dark funnel and transformed into a wolf with fur as black as coal. Theo could feel the dark energy penetrating into his pores like a million electrical pulses. As she crouched, ready to attack, Magda's red eyes glared at him and Diva with hatred as intense as the evil he'd experienced from Zlo. Despite his bravery, he shuddered.

Magda's aim was to kill.

"*I've got this*," Diva thought to him. "*Magda and I have some issues to resolve.*"

Before Theo could reply or move, Diva pounced like a wildcat. With two leaps, she stood before Magda.

Theo followed quickly behind, to be there if his sister needed help. Magda had so maligned Diva, that he understood her desire to put a stop to their aunt's lies and treachery.

"I could make this even and turn into a wolf, too," Diva shouted at Magda. "Or we can battle in human form. It's your choice."

Magda growled as if thinking about what gave her the advantage. She spun around in circles, like a dog chasing its tail. The black mist swirled all around her. When it dissolved, she'd reverted to a woman dressed in black. She twisted her golden bracelet, and swarms of snakes materialized from the ground.

Diva snorted. "You think your magic outshines that which the Colobari gave us?"

Theo wanted to add that Magda had failed to achieve the priests' level of power, but he remained silent. This was Diva's battle, and she had no need to fight with words.

Diva pointed the staff toward the snakes that slithered toward her. They burst into flames. Next, she held the staff in Magda's direction. "Admit your defeat, and we'll be lenient with your punishment."

Magda paled and trembled, but said, "Never!"

The word had barely left her lips when a silver net sailed over her, knocking her to the ground.

Theo looked to see who had thrown it. One of the Knights of Darkness wiped his hands together as if removing offending dirt.

He kneeled and bowed his head. The other Knights surrounded Radan and Bor Stobor. Spears kept the traitors hemmed in.

Magda screamed and thrashed on the ground, but the net prevented her escape.

Ignoring his aunt, Theo approached the kneeling Knight. "You would betray her? Why?"

The man kept his head bowed. "My Knights of Darkness and I are ready to serve the new king and queen of Zmeykovo. Our hearts were tempted by the power Zlo offered. Too late, we saw the destruction he planned. By then, his enchantment held us captive. We are free now that he is gone. Our hearts are tainted, so we cannot return to being esteemed Knights of Light, but we wish to serve in whatever way you will have us."

Diva pointed her staff toward the kneeling man. A white light surrounded him, and then faded. "He speaks the truth."

"Stand up," Theo commanded, and the man obeyed. "I've read a book called *Lodge of Light and Lodge of Darkness*. In the past, both houses existed. The book explained how light and darkness are both needed for growth and renewal. We, Diva and I, and all of Zmeykovo, will be honored to have both lodges restored and working together again."

Diva squeezed Theo's arm. "And your first official duty will be to escort Magda, Radan, and Bor Stobor to the prison."

"One question before you go," Theo said. "How did you get the net?"

The man grinned. "The leader of the water creatures was howling up a storm, making promises of wealth to anyone who freed him."

"So, you took him up on his offer?" Theo asked.

"In a way," the man said. "I watched him squirm for a while before I freed him. The only reward I asked was that he be gentler with his children. None of us likes a brute. I kept the net after I released him to keep it out of his greedy paws."

"Good thinking. Before you take my aunt away, I want a few words with her." Theo strode toward Magda.

She snarled. "The crown is rightfully mine. My medallion, which you stole, claims me to be the one born to rule."

"A lie," Theo said. "You had to be with Zunitza when the two of you hid the crown. We found Hala's note under the pouch the crown was in."

Magda blinked and went silent before she murmured more to herself than to Theo, "My sister put the letter there? That's why I couldn't find it."

"Yes," Diva said as she joined Theo. "In a journal."

"You!" Magda growled at Diva. "It's all your fault. You should have died in the demon forest. Then the medallion and its promise would have been mine."

Theo snorted. "What are you talking about? The letter didn't say anything about that."

"Of course not," she shot back. "Why would Hala mention that part of her vision if you were dead? She did address the letter to the two of you, after all. If you were dead, you couldn't ever read it."

"You're sick." Theo's stomach churned.

Jealousy had nothing to do with Magda leaving the infant Diva in the demon forest. It had always been his aunt's obsession with power and desire to rule.

"Did my mother know this?" he asked.

"No. Do you think she would have let me anywhere near her while she was pregnant if she did?" Magda laughed. "I overheard Hala when she was speaking with the Colobari about her vision, wondering what to do."

Theo shook his head and walked away. "Get Magda out of here now," he said to the Knight. "I can't stand looking at her."

LATER THAT EVENING, Theo and Diva stood on a castle balcony. The celebration by the lake had been interrupted, so they would speak to the people, their people, from here.

Diva looked like a queen, dressed in royal robes and wearing the queen's crown. The crowd quieted as she stepped to the edge of the balcony.

"People of Zmeykovo," she began. "The road behind us has been difficult. For some, like me, this reign of terror is all we have known."

Gentle murmurs drifted throughout the crowd as people nodded and acknowledged her words.

"None of us knows what tomorrow will bring," Diva continued. "The Colobari see many events, but no one future is certain. Theo and I"—She dragged him to her side, and the people cheered—"we have done what had to be done to rid this land of the menace that has plagued it for too long. We will continue to face whatever challenges lie ahead and will do everything within our power to keep you safe—whether the road ahead is easy or difficult."

A thunderous uproar spread throughout the people. Diva raised her hands, and the noise dwindled.

"Not only that, but we will rebuild Zmeykovo, restore it to its former beauty," Diva began. "I want to build more libraries, make our history known to all. Your children and their children should treasure the knowledge of our land. It must be preserved for generations to come."

"Hear, hear." Jabalaka's voice rose above the others.

"As you know," she said while she squeezed Theo's hand, "your king was not raised here, even though Zmeykovo royal blood runs through his veins."

Murmurs drifted throughout the crowd once more.

"Theo would like to address his own concerns with you." Diva stepped back, leaving Theo to face the crowd.

"I have come to know and love Zmeykovo as my home." His voice cracked, and he paused. "But I also have a family in the human world. A mother who raised me and a sister who shared the good and bad times. I have a duty to them as well as to you."

Not a peep came out of the crowd. All eyes stared at him intently. Theo didn't know who was more scared about what he was going to say. Them or him. Diva was their beloved queen. They knew she would never desert them. But they didn't know his plans.

"Things are different in the human world," Theo continued. "Most people there don't believe places like Zmeykovo exist."

That stirred a few comments among those gathered: "That's unbelievable," "How rude," and "Well, they don't exist for me either." Other people had once come from the human world, and their thoughts were those of both missing home and glad that they had left.

"I'm not sure I want the world to know this wonderful place exists," Theo said. "Zmeykovo would be overrun with humans, many who might try to take control like Lamia and Zlo."

Angry shouts and screams echoed among the people.

When the sounds stopped, Theo cleared his throat. "I have no doubt I will find a balance with taking care of my family in Selo and being with everyone here. You will not be alone. I will return as often as I can. And Diva can summon me if any danger threatens Zmeykovo again."

At the mention of Diva's name, cheers spread through the crowd.

"You are my people, and I will always fight to defend you and our land against all threats. Our strength is in being united. Together, we can overcome any obstacle." Theo stepped back and breathed a sigh of relief.

The cheers of the crowd were deafening.

When Theo finished speaking, Sur and his herd soared into the air with Samodivi riders. A trail of sparkling dust lit the sky like fireworks. The forest became alive with singing, chittering, bellowing animals. The sounds somehow merged into a harmonious whole. In the meadow, people danced and sang around bonfires. The reaction of everyone, their love and devotion of their leaders, especially their beloved queen, Diva, touched Theo's heart.

The day's ceremony had finally come to an end. The memory would remain with him forever, and he was sure Diva felt the same.

"You did great." She hugged him. "Everyone loves you as much as they do me, and our land is free once again."

"It is. But with such a great loss." Theo sighed. Zmey's death weighed heavy on his heart.

"I miss him, too," Diva said, knowing what Theo was feeling. "I barely got to know him as my father."

Pavel stepped onto the balcony from the room where he'd been waiting. "Look." He pointed to the sky.

Once more a rainbow surrounded by silver dust appeared. Zunitza's voice spoke to both Theo's and Diva's minds. *"My children. I'm so proud of you. Your father is proud of you, too."*

Silver dust sprinkled over them.

"I feel strange." Diva closed her eyes. "I just felt Zmey touch my arm, and a surge of energy went through me."

She opened her eyes.

"Diva!" Pavel grabbed her arms. "Your eyes are glowing."

"And my hands, too." She held them up.

Colors shimmered around her fingertips. Blue. Then green. Then purple. And more. The colors kept changing.

"What's happening to you?" Pavel asked.

Theo examined Diva's hands. "I think she's gaining her dragon powers."

As they watched, Diva transformed into a beautiful dragon, like a butterfly emerging from its cocoon. Her scales and wings shone with iridescent colors that sparkled like the ocean on a moonlit night.

"Do you think you can fly as a dragon?" Theo asked her.

"I'm going to try," she said to his mind.

"Then let's show our people what we can do." Theo shifted into a red dragon.

Brother and sister, magnificent dragons, soared to the sky. Gasps, then cheers, came from the people. Two sets of dragon wings beat in unison as the siblings flew over the entirety of their land. They beheld the bustle of activity in Samodivi Fortress. They circled the Znahar Tree and breathed fire as a greeting to

Kosara. At Rusalki Bay, the two dragons dipped down low and let their feet skim through the water. They flew over the Cold Marsh, the Forest of Whispering Bells, and the Kukeri sanctuary.

They rejoiced in the peace that had settled everywhere. Brother and sister circled the land once more, nudging each other with their snouts. They had fought hard to free the land of the evil that had threatened to destroy it. Now it was time to play, to revel in their victory. They raced through the clouds, dove and soared over the mountains, and hovered over valleys.

As they neared the castle on their return trip, two amazing sights met their eyes. A golden dome shimmered to life over Kaleto. The Colobari had kept their promise. The Ispolini could live in peace from the rest of Zmeykovo.

Theo was happy for the giants, but it made him sad. He felt Diva's sadness, too.

"Do you think they'll ever change their minds?" he asked. *"Or will they be enemies of dragons forever?"*

"I think one day they'll seek us out," she replied. *"Remember how they looked at the two of us? It wasn't the same way they reacted to Zmey."*

Diva was right. It was as if the Ispolini weren't sure if he and Diva were dragons or not. The look was one of curiosity. He hoped that meant one day a new relationship would develop between dragons and giants. For now, he dipped his wings in their direction to wish the Ispolini well.

The second wonder was a new star that shown red and blue above their homeland. Zmey and his sister were joined in peace and forgiveness. They would watch over the land below for eternity.

AN ENTRY IN *The Chronicle of Zmeykovo*, dated many years later:

Our young hero king and his faithful friend did finally return to the human world, but they came often to Zmeykovo. After our hero king reached the age of maturity, he remained in our land, frequently bringing his human mother and sister for extended visits. Our hero's friend made his home in our land, as well.

The adventures of our young heroes, brother and sister and friend, were far from over. Under the rule of Zmey and Zunitza's offspring, the land flourished and people prospered. The young rulers provided much wisdom to those who sought it. They had each other and the support of the people. Together, they continued to fight for the freedom and safety of their beloved homeland.

The star that was born that night was given the name Ouroboros Star. Brother and sister, fallen in battle, were united once more in the sky. It twinkles red and blue even now to remind us hope exists and love is powerful, even in the darkest of times.

About the Author

Ronesa Aveela is "the creative power of two." Two authors, that is. Nelly, the main force behind the work, the creative genius, was born in Bulgaria and moved to the U.S. in the 1990s. She grew up with stories of wild Samodivi, Kikimora, the dragons Zmey and Lamia, Baba Yaga, and much more. She's a freelance artist and writer. She likes writing mystery romance inspired by legends and tales. In her free time, she paints. Her artistic interests include the female figure, Greek and Thracian mythology, folklore tales, and the natural world interpreted through her eyes. She is married and has two children.

Rebecca, her writing partner was born and raised in the New England area. She has a background in writing and editing, as well as having a love of all things from different cultures. She's learned so much about Bulgarian culture, folklore, and rituals, and writes to share that knowledge with others.

Connect with us at www.ronesaaveela.com.
Be sure to follow us on Kickstarter for extra goodies when we launch new books: https://www.kickstarter.com/profile/ronesa-aveela/.

Dragon Village Series

1) *The Unborn Hero of Dragon Village*
2) *Dragon Village Firebird*
3) *Dragon Village Ouroboros*
4) *Dragon Village Golden Apple*
5) *Dragon Village Colobar*

Special Offer

Would you like to learn more about folklore and mythology? Sign up for our newsletter and receive a FREE supplement to our "Spirits and Creatures" book series. To download the article about a malicious water spirit, Vodyanoy or Vodnik, use this link: https://BookHip.com/VFVPQJ or find the link on our website.

Further Reading

Discover more about the dragons and other creatures in this book in our nonfiction series called "Spirits and Creatures." Available in ebook, paperback, and hardcopy formats from your favorite retailer. You can also request your local library to carry a copy.

Household Spirits – https://books2read.com/household-spirits
Rusalki – Slavic Mermaids – https://books2read.com/rusalki
Dragons – https://books2read.com/dragons-aveela
Baba Yaga – https://books2read.com/babayaga
More to come…